SADIE

KENSINGTON COVE

MICHELLE DE LA GARZA

ACKNOWLEDGMENTS

This book wouldn't have been possible without the support and encouragement of the many people who saw me through this wondrous and emerging process. I would like to thank my family for their unwavering support and dedication, and my editor and partner in crime, who always has a word list or two for me.

For my daughter, Kristin,
Who inspires me to be more than I am;
My husband, Valdemar,
Who is my guiding light and soulmate;
Sons, Patrick and Joshua,
Who offer a ray of light in the darkness.

**Want more Kensington Cove
Click here to sign up for the Newsletter.**

Sadie Reed never knew her real family, but a series of chaotic events sends her running to Kensington Cove. The day she arrives, a driving mishap lands her in the arms of one hot, sexy, leather-clad biker, Ethan Cotter.

Lupine shifter Ethan Cotter, a member of the Shoshone clan, has a problem. And that curvaceous problem, with long, tantalizing legs has a name, Sadie Reed.

The wolf in him stirred the moment they met. But Ethan's worried his secret will scare her off. But Sadie has secrets of her own, secrets that will turn Kensington Cove into a battle zone for supremacy.

CONTENTS

CHAPTER ONE

Sadie Reed

"TURN RIGHT." The cell phone's navigation system pierces the interior silence of the Infinity that's coasting in the dark, over an unfamiliar rural Texas road.

Fingers wrapped tightly around the wheel, I take a sharp right.

"Would it kill ya to give an advance notice next time?"

The car's bald, smooth tires screech over the pitted two-lane road, then skid off the shoulder for a few seconds.

My backpack purse topples over and lands on the floorboard, spilling the contents.

"Oh, great. That's just great!"

A quick glance in the rearview mirror reveals an undisturbed pile of clothes on the backseat.

My cell rings. Dana Moore, brown hair and freckles, flashes across the screen.

"Hey, Freckles. What's up?"

"Where the hell are you?" Dana's bubbly voice oozes through the phone. "We're at the Sonic on Main and 4th Street."

"Yeah. Don't wait on me." Dana, Lynn, Megan, and the rest of the gang's voices merge together in the background to form one loud, unintelligible crackling of speech.

"Why not?" The whine in Dana's voice brings to mind pouty lips—most likely tinted with blue, purple, or green— well, anything bright and up in your face.

"Moving."

"Damn. That's today? Man, that sucks. I have tickets to *South by South West* tonight. Now what am I supposed to do?"

"Jeez, didn't mean to ruin *your* day. It's not as if people forced you to move to a shit hole."

"Sorry, girl." The noise in the background fades. "I guess I didn't put the right moving day on the agenda." She sniffles.

It hadn't been on my agenda either. Hell, I still had things to do, places to go, and people to visit in San Antonio, Texas, or at least, who I wanted to see—Dana, namely.

"It's not you. They changed the moving date—had to leave three weeks early."

A deer leaps out of the tall grass and sprints in front of the car.

"What the fuck?" I grab the wheel and swerve off the road and on to the edge of the shoulder.

"You okay?"

"Yeah." My heart hammers in my chest, battering ribs like a snare drum. "I'm fine."

"What happened?"

"Bambi ran across the fucking road."

"Oh, my God. That's so cool."

"Yeah, no." That's so like her to say. "It really wasn't."

"Hey, so what happened? Why'd the date get changed?"

"Dr. Gus called me into the office this morning."

"The counselor or principle?"

"Counselor." An image of Dr. Gus, the principle, in her business suit next to her counselor husband, fill my thoughts. "Anyway, he said, *'There's been a development,'* then gushed about how sorry he was, and how things always happen for a reason."

"That's bullshit?"

"I know, right? It's not as if *his* life has gone from semi-crap to, well, a healthy heaping of shit running downhill."

"What an ass. So, what was the development? Did he say?"

"He mumbled something about the Greene household and their dealings."

"Isn't that your foster family?"

"Was. They were illegally using government funds—for drugs mainly, I think."

"It's not as if their dealings were a secret or anything. Everyone on the block knows that. Hell, I knew. Those who didn't, chose not to know."

"Yep. Drones." Plowed pastures fan out as far as the eye can see on both sides of the car. "Sticking their heads in the sand and living in a make-believe world."

"So, where are you moving now?"

"A ranch, in Kensington Cove. But it's different."

"Different how?" Dana squeals into the phone. A male voice filters into the background.

"Is that you, Matt?"

"Yep, and Dana is indisposed of for the next hour or

two." Matt's voice booms over the cell. "She'll have to call you back." The line goes dead.

"Well, that's great. Just fuckin' great."

Growing up in the foster care system teaches one to never count on staying in one place for too long, which suits me fine, but now, things are different.

Where I'm heading this time leads to home—to a family ranch, roots unknown to me, which is cool but scary as hell. Something I'm not sure how to feel about yet.

If the Greene family hadn't walked into incarceration, I could've eased into a new life at the end of the school year, but no, they had to deal some homegrown shit to a police officer, and I'm the one punished, forced to move away from my school, my friends.

The cell rings again. This time, *Attorney* flashes across the screen.

"Hello."

"Hi, Sadie. This is Mr. Lambert."

I glance at my phone but can't see the GPS location screen to see how far away the town is now.

"I'm still on I-10, but I don't think I'm far. When I get to the burger joint, where do I go? Front? Back?"

"There's been a change of plans."

"What do you mean?"

"I'm tied up in court and can't leave right now. I've phoned ahead, and someone will meet you at the ranch house later tonight. Just use the keys to get in."

"Where's that?" Blood rushed to my ears, making it hard to concentrate, let alone hear.

"Don't panic." Static crackles over the line.

"Hello? Are you there? Can you hear me?"

"Yeah. I'm here. Don't stress. You've got the address in

the paperwork I sent over." He pauses. "Hey, they just called my case."

"Wait. I need—"

"I'll call later. Gotta go."

The line drops, and the GPS directions open on the screen.

Sixteen years in the system without a card, a call, or a simple *'Hi, how are you?'* from any family member, and now, there's a lead on my ancestral line. A long-lost relative —unfucking believable.

Well, at least this time, I'm moving to my place instead of leaving someone else's, and like he said, I got the paperwork to prove it.

The cell, perched inside the cracked phone holder, shows the next turn is nine-tenths of a mile away.

My stomach gurgles and butterflies bounce around. At this point, I can't tell if it's from hunger or the stress of the unknown.

A farmhouse, barn, and corral sit on the property in good condition, at least from the aerial photos. Some quick internet searches before I left, brought up indigenous wildlife: turkeys, armadillos—which carry bacteria causing leprosy, or so an article had said—deer, snapping turtles, wild pigs, raccoons, rabbits, and bobcats, as well as mountain lions, coyotes, and gray wolves that all inhabit the area.

The thought of running into hunting pack-animals, carnivores, does nothing for me.

Hell, I'd rather find a group of leprosy-dillos than entertain a pack of large cats or wolves.

The road ahead twists and turns.

Nothing but brush and moonlight surrounds me.

A few fireflies, or what I hope are fireflies and not eyes, glow in the thicket close to the shoulder.

The headlights of my car illuminate a green reflective sign.

"Kensington Cove city limits." Population stats, nine hundred and ninety-one, flash before my eyes. "You really are a shit hole, aren't you?"

CHAPTER TWO

Ethan Cotter

THE METALLIC SCENT of blood lingers, and the coppery taste coats my tongue and mouth, which only serves to wake my inner beast. On edge, I scan the area. But it's not the blood that holds my attention. No. It's the residual stench of an unknown lycan that sets my predatory instincts on heightened alert.

Kneeling, I inspect the slash marks carved into the abdomens and necks of the two mutilated calves.

A familiar scent lingers in the air. It belongs to a human rancher.

"Howdy, Jeb." Head down, I continue examining the specimens.

Two sets of legs, eight in all, protrude from a single birthing sack. The outer shell of the tiny hooves, still soft, feel like rubber bands.

"Did you know she was carrying twins?"

"Yeah." Jeb Snyder spits a wad of snuff-infused saliva. "I suspected as much a little over a month ago."

"They're small, even for newborns."

"Betty here wasn't due to give birth for another couple of weeks." Jeb pats the cow's neck, then loops a rope around her head. "Isn't that right, 'ol girl?"

"How'd you find them?"

"When Betty didn't come home, I went looking for her." Jeb coils the rope around his calloused hand, taking out the slack. "This is the second attack on my property in as many weeks. Plus, the Taylors had a colt taken down just five days ago."

"I heard about that."

"Well, a few of us landowners are thinking of getting together and hunting the animal who did this. You and your brother are welcome to join us." He pauses. "It sure is a shame." Jeb shakes his head. "As a rancher, you expect a loss now and then when food is scarce but that ain't the case here. No. This animal isn't hunting for food. Nope. It's killing for the sport."

The phone in my pocket vibrates against my leg. Rising, I fish the device free, and then check the call log.

Cole's number sprawls across the screen. He's my older brother—or parental shadow, as I like to refer to him.

"What?" Fourteen months separates us, but you'd think it was more with the way he rides my ass.

Ever since Dad's death a few months ago, Ma says he's seventeen going on forty—he sure as hell has the grumpy old man part down.

"What'd you find out?" Cole's voice booms in my ear. "Was it a coyote?"

"Nope. Afraid not." I walk away from Jeb.

No sense in a human overhearing the conversation. The content isn't meant for his kind's ears.

"Lycan?" asks Cole in his, I'm-in-charge-voice.

"Yep." I duck under the barbed-wire fence.

"You leaving?" Jeb leads Betty to the edge of his property. He leans against a post.

"Yeah. Ma expects me home for supper." I head to my motorcycle parked on the shoulder of the road.

"Say hello to your mother."

"I will. Let me know when you rally the other ranchers," I shout over a shoulder at Jeb. "You have my number."

"I'll give you a call."

The sun is setting, and soon, it'll be dark.

I mount my bike, then heads off down the road.

Drawing in a deep breath, I catch traces of the lycan.

Fucking rogue asshole, the words rolls around in my head.

Kensington Cove has always had visiting lupines and lycans. But here lately, the town has had more than its fair share of both, especially lycans without a clan. And the Kweo are always more than willing to add another stray to their cause, which is what makes *that* clan unpredictable, unlike my brethren, the Shoshone.

Hell. If it were up to the Alpha of the Kweo, the masquerade would've ended long ago.

Shadows of darkness dance around.

I flip on the headlight and zip my leather jacket.

A single beam cuts through the night.

In the distance, the lights of a car peek over the hill. It swerves, and its headlights flicker.

"Fucking kids," I breathe under my breath.

For the last several months, a group of human teens have

made the trip down the road to park at The Point—a bluff overlooking the town. A situation Cole and I will have to remedy much sooner than later because of the rogue stray.

I slow at the private entrance to my property, then stop.

The twin headlights continue to blink on the winding road.

"Fuck."

Cole will bitch if I don't do something about them.

In the twilight of the early evening, I pull out and set a course to intercept the teens.

CHAPTER THREE

Sadie Reed

"SIGNAL LOST." The electronic voice grates on my last nerve. Well, along with the fact the asshat-of-an-attorney bailed on me.

"What the hell?"

I rip the phone free of the docking station.

"Are you freakin' kidding me? How the hell are there no bars?"

A quick push of the button on the side of the device starts a reboot.

Come on. Come on. You piece of shit."

The phone vibrates, and the logo flashes across the screen.

A horn blares in my ears.

Looking up, a single headlight shines in my eyes. The phone slips out of my grasp and tumbles to the floorboard under my feet.

"Fuck." I swerve to miss the oncoming light and end up in a ditch.

I slam the car in park, leaving the engine running.

Eyes closed, I press the back of my head against the seat and will the pounding of my heart to recede.

A rap on the window makes me jump.

My eyes fly open.

"Hey." A guy stoops next to the car. "You in there." He motions for me to roll down the window.

I shake my head. "Uhm . . . I'm okay." Alone, on a deserted road in the dark, with a stranger isn't exactly the place I want to be.

Flashes of a news headline roll through my head; *tonight, at ten, a teen slain on a country road.*

The thought makes my stomach churn, and an uneasiness washes over me.

Moonlight catches the contours of the leather-clad guy's face. Light stubble lines his jaw, and his sun-tanned face has a natural glow.

He taps the window, again. "Roll it down."

My hand hovers over the control panel. *Fucking attorney.*

I glance at the floorboard.

The grip of the handgun I swiped from Mr. Greene peeks out from under the seat and glistens in the moonlight.

"I don't have all night." His voice has a low, throaty pitch to it, almost a growl.

"Just a minute." I press a finger against the lever and roll the window a third of the way down.

"Are you okay?" His voice is deep. It has a baritone ring to it.

"Yeah." I glance up.

If guessing, he seems my age, maybe older, but not by much—high school age.

There's something about the tone that puts me at ease, and the tension in my shoulders roll away.

"What about you?" The thought of almost hitting someone on a motorcycle, because I was attending to my stupid phone instead of the road, makes the muscles in my abdomen contract.

He nods once. "Good. Then do you mind telling me what the *hell* you were doing in the middle of the road?"

"Excuse me?" Tension creeps up into my neck and shoulders.

"Do I need to repeat the question?"

"My GPS lost connection." I swallow hard. "It was restarting." A cold sweat lines my brow. Nervously, I wipe my sweaty palms on my skirt. "Uhm, I guess I veered out of the lane."

Staring at the stranger, I'm unable to read him, which is odd. Usually, I'm quick to make a decision, and generally, my choice is a solid one and spot on.

"You think?"

"Look. I'm sorry." I cast my eyes down, avoiding his probing stare. The tip of my index finger rests on the window control. "I didn't mean to—"

"—I haven't seen you around before. Where're you headed?"

"Kensington Cove."

"Are you moving?"

"What?"

"The clothes in the back." He holds my gaze.

"Yeah." My grip on the wheel tightens.

"So, you have family in town?"

"Something like that."

He rubs his jaw, then clears his throat. "Are you stuck?"

"What?"

"The car? Are you stuck in the mud?"

"Oh, I don't think so."

He glances at the tires, shakes his head, and then backs away from the car. "If you have enough traction to pull out of the ditch, I'll show you where the turn is."

Mist covers the window, hindering my view.

A dog or wolf howls in the distances, and the fine hairs on the nape of my neck stand on end.

"Please, don't be stuck." I slide the gear in drive and give the car gas.

The tires spin, sending a geyser of mud spewing into the air. I back off the gas, then try it again.

"Stop." He walks to the car and taps the hood. "You're not going anywhere in this tonight."

I slide the car into park. "Shit," I say, barely above a whisper.

Leaning over, I pick up my phone.

"Zero bars, really? Great. Stranded out in the middle of nowhere with nothing around but a guy in leather." I flip on the windshield wipers, then follow his movements.

"You're gonna need a tow. But at least it starts." He makes his way around the front of the bumper which is held together by duct tape and bungee rope. "Where'd you get this death trap?"

"Craig's List. I scooped ice cream all summer to buy it."

Why the hell did I tell him that? It's not like he needs my life story.

"It's dark." I glance around for signs, mile markers, or any connection to civilization, but come up empty-handed.

"Yeah." He cracks a grin and a dimple in his left cheek winks. "Usually is at night."

"Well, hell, lookie here, I got myself a real comedian." I resist the urge to roll my eyes. "I meant I don't see any city lights."

"What's your name?" He stoops close to the opened window.

I hesitate, unsure if I should answer the question or not, and then blurt out, "Sadie. Sadie Reed."

Way to go. Tell the killer comedian your name, idiot.

"I'm Ethan Cotter." A single eyebrow shoots up in amusement. "The way I see it, I can give you a lift, or you can stay here with no reception." He leans in through the window.

Another howl reverberates. But this time, the call is closer.

My eyes widen, and I swallow hard. "Was that a dog, coyote . . . wolf?

"A gray wolf. Come on, and I'll give you a lift, city girl."

I lock gazes with him. His eyes. They're a piercing grayish blue. I hadn't noticed before.

"And don't worry, I won't bite unless you want me to."

A small wolfish grin washes across his lips, exposing a row of straight, white teeth.

"Yeah. Thanks. That's reassuring."

"So, what's it going to be, Sadie Reed? Are you staying —or what?"

I take a deep breath, pause to think, and then grab my keys. Reaching over the seat, I scoop up the contents of my purse—gun and all—then open the door.

CHAPTER FOUR

Ethan Cotter

LONG LEGS connected to a well-defined body step out of the Infinity. Once standing, the owner of the legs tugs on the black flowing skirt that covers half of her bare, milky-white thighs.

For her short stature, hers go on for miles and demand my full attention. My eyes travel the length of her frame, starting with her white tennis shoes and short socks.

The curve of her calves flows to supple, trim knees that lead to the tone, muscular, mouthwatering thighs I can't tear my eyes from.

Thighs I like to wrap my arms around.

"Fuck," I breathe under my breath. Fluid, more like drool, builds in my mouth, forcing me to swallow.

Get a grip, man, and stop salivating, I tell my inner wolf.

I take in the form-fitted blue tank top hugging her athletic body.

The wolf inside me continues to stir. It can hear the erratic heartbeats pounding in her chest.

A palatable mixture of fear and faint arousal swirl in the air, driving my beast to the edge of a frenzy. At this moment, all it wants is to smell her, taste her, to stake a claim to what it desires.

"Come on." I smack my lips, relishing the savory taste. "It's getting darker."

"Uh, okay." She checks the driver's side door, once, twice, three times.

"Yeah. It's locked already."

Nervous energy flows from her pores, making her fidgety.

"My stuff's in the back. What if someone—"

"No one will mess with it." I slow my pace, allowing her to take a step in front of me. "So, don't stress."

"It's all I have." Her voice cracks, revealing a layer of vulnerability that draws my inner beast closer.

"Where'd you say you came from?"

She swallows hard. "I didn't." Apprehension builds a wall between me and her and raises her tension level.

A glance over my shoulder reveals an old, fraying bumper sticker, 'Julian Castro' for mayor.

San Antonio, Texas—I was right, a city girl.

On the walk to the bike, my eyes drink in the sway of her hips. The rhythmic motion draws my inner beast in for a closer view.

Above the crease of the back of her knee, a birthmark with fluted, petal like edges offers a sharp contrast to her pale flesh.

Is it even or ridged? My tongue tingles at the thought of caressing the borders.

The wind gusts pick up, swishing her skirt against her thighs.

She smooths out the fabric and struggles to hold it down.

A mist covers her body and goosebumps erupt on her skin.

Humans run cooler than lupines and lose more of their warmth in the cold—an event that in my youth often left me perplexed.

"Cold?" My beast picks up her increased respirations, and zeros in on her trembling, lower lip.

"Yeah." She adjusts the strap of her backpack purse. The weight sends the strap of her tank sliding over her shoulder, revealing a pink sports bra.

My canines ache under the gumline, begging for release, and I struggle to remain in control.

Back off, I tell my inner wolf. *What the hell, man?*

I've never wanted to bite anyone or anything, and now, five minutes after meeting City, my beast wants to mark her.

"Put it on." I slide my jacket off. "Trust me. You'll need it more than me."

She hesitates, takes the garment from my hand, and then slips it on. "Thanks." A faint flush brings color to her cheeks.

"Welcome."

The cuffs hang below her fingertips, but she rolls them to her wrists, revealing slender fingers without jewelry.

Not taken. My inner beast stirs.

"I didn't think it'd be chilly this week, well, today."

She's about five-foot, six inches with a toned build, which is just how I like my females.

"That's Texas weather for you." I mount the bike. "Hop on." With a wave of a hand, I motion for her to sit.

"You don't wear a helmet?" Her growing fear lingers in the air, and my beast sips on it.

"No. Never have, but I've never needed one, either." My eyes rake up and down her body.

The wolf continues to drink in her alluring scent, which makes my dick stir.

"Have you ever been on a bike before?" I've never smelled something or someone as sweet and tantalizing as this little morsel.

"No." She shakes her head, then nervously bites her lower lip. "Well, a dirt bike. Does that count?"

"Not so much." I wink and continue to struggle to maintain control. "I'll take it slow. Promise."

Slow isn't what me or my beast wants right now. And in defiance, the wolf silently howls, demanding release.

"Okay." She fidgets with the zipper and bites down on her lower lip once more.

A low, throaty growl escapes my mouth because I'd like to be the one nibbling on that full, lush lip. And right now, all the beast wants to do—what I want to do—is draw her into my arms and possess her. Well, that and hold her hips steady as I . . .

Fuck. Get a grip on your inner beast, I think to myself.

"Need some help?" I can't peel my eyes away from her legs.

"I think I can—"

I reigh in the wolf's libido, which now has my dick standing at attention and begging.

"Let me." Reaching out, I take hold of the bottom of the leather jacket—my jacket—which she's now wearing, and I coax her closer to my frame. "There's a trick to it."

She palms my forearms, steading herself, and I relish her warmth.

"Is it safe to be on the road?" Her eyes widen like a doe caught in a crossbeam of headlights. "You know, with the weather and all?" She blinks several times. "If it's not far, we could walk, right?"

"Not a good idea." Thoughts of the rogue lupine invade my mind. "Country life is far different from the city after dark."

"Oh." She parses her lips.

I zip the garment, covering the curves of her breasts and then snap the lower section of the waistband that falls well below her hips.

"Come on. It's getting darker and wetter."

Sadie takes in a deep breath, then sighs. "There's a first time for everything." Tentatively, she straddles the bike. "Or so I've heard."

She scoots back as far as she can, but not before her skirt exposes even more of her thighs.

Tugging at the fabric, she wiggles in the seat, trying to cover her legs.

"I already told you." A chuckle escapes my lips. "I won't bite unless you want me to."

Fuck. What the hell's wrong with me?

I shouldn't be toying with her like this. It's not as if she understands what it means to be marked or claimed by a wolf—to be someone's mate. But if she knew what I was, what I was capable of, she'd run the other way and never look back.

"You're going to have to hold on to me." I grab one of her hands and place it on my waist.

The contact makes my body buzz.

When I start the engine, she jumps and clings to the sides of my T-shirt.

"Have you ever, you know, wrecked?"

"No. Now, scoot up, so you don't fall off."

Sadie inches near but keeps a respectable distance from my frame.

"More." The beast within lurks. Anticipation builds. "So, you can wrap your arms around my waist."

She wiggles on the seat, drawing closer, and then laces her fingers above my navel.

"That's it." I draw in a deep breath, relishing her scent.

Pulling on to the road, I gradually increase the speed, giving her time to adjust to the movement of the bike.

"This isn't so bad." A carefree giggle passes her lips.

The road ahead winds around.

"Hold on tight." I approach the first deep curve, and Sadie slides up the seat.

She wraps her arms around my waist, pressing her warm thighs, abdomen, and breasts against my frame. Her body molds to mine, and the sweet aroma of her growing arousal replaces the fear of the unknown.

"*Got you.*" The wolf inside me grins.

CHAPTER FIVE

Sadie Reed

WHISPS OF HIS HAIR tickle my face.

He smells like earth; woody, musky, coconutty, with a hint of patchouli, star anise, tonka bean, and vanilla.

On the open road, I feel free, unburdened by the strings of my former life.

Live in the future, I think to myself, *and leave the past where it belongs.*

The vibration of the power between my legs sends a shiver the length of my spine.

"You doin' okay?" The rich undertones of his voice cuts through the sound of the revving engine.

"Oh, my God." A squeal leaves my lips. "I'm more than okay."

Riding on the back of the motorcycle is exhilarating but frightening at the same time.

I've been on dirt bikes before, but nothing, thus far, compares to the thrill of riding on the open road.

Well, on a motorcycle with a hot guy with rock hard abs.

He comes to another turn, rounds the corner, and my grip on his shirt slips, and my butt slides across the smooth leather of the seat.

Fear shoots through me.

"Hold on tight." One handed, he steers, placing the other behind him, cradling me to his back.

I squeeze my thighs, pressing them against his jeans. Wrapping my arms around him, my hands slide under the hem of his shirt.

My fingers grip his abdomen.

His muscles ripple and contract under my touch, making the tips of my fingers sensitive and tingle.

I feel a pull in my belly as if hundreds of butterfly wings take flight, fluttering about. Something's happening, I can feel it.

The guy, the bike, the mist—my mind wanders—somehow, it all seems familiar, but it can't be.

Yet, I feel a connection akin to *déjà vu*. It's as if on this hour, this day, this moment, fate intervened, bringing me and him together as one.

Great. Now I sound like a mystic eight ball.

My fingers fan over his right peck. A nail grazes his nipple, and he takes in a sharp breath.

A low, throaty growl reverberates deep in his chest.

The sound makes my heart flutter, and a small smile graces my lips.

At least now, I know I'm not the only one who feels the strong sexual pull.

Ethan comes to a three-way stop.

I wobble on the seat and move a leg. Toes pointed. I reach for the asphalt.

"No. Keep your foot on the peg." He slides a hand

across the side of my thigh, holding me in place. "Or you'll throw off the balance."

"Sorry." I raise my leg and rest the sole of my shoe on the peg, once again.

"Don't be." His touch makes me acutely aware of how intimately I'm pressed against him. "Now, you know."

When he relinquishes his hold, he brushes the tips of his fingers up the side of my thigh, and my skin erupts in goosebumps.

"Uhm. It's dark." The mist, now replaced by rain, hinders my visibility. "I don't see any lights yet."

"So, you gonna tell me where you're from, or do I need to guess?"

"San Antonio, Texas."

"Well, you won't find any city lights out here, at least, not until we're closer to town, which is that way." He points to the highway. "And even those are minute." He pauses. "So, Sadie Reed, what's our destination?" His voice is thick and desire-ridden.

"What?"

"Who're you visiting in Kensington Cove? Where are we going?"

"Actually, it's not in the city. It's the Novak Ranch."

Ethan glances over his shoulder, and his brows shoot up. "You don't say?"

He takes off, and shards of rain blow in my face. I press my cheek against his back, using him as a shield.

Drawing in a deep breath, I breathe in his scent. Even in the rain, that earthy aroma exudes undiluted from his body. It's a smell I could get used to really quick.

After turning down a gravel road, Ethan travels another three-quarters of a mile. A line of trees—mainly oak, ash, and cedar, which led to dense forest—line the packed caliche path.

In the city, the rain smells of diluted exhaust, trash, and the meat packing plant near the apartments I lived in with the Greene family.

"It's just over the hill." Wind howls through the trees, making it hard to hear his voice.

The top of the incline provides a glimpse of a fog-infused clearing. A faint outline of a roof appears followed by a large building.

Fog, thick and wet to the touch, lingers, making the air heavy.

"Why's it so dark?"

At the end of the driveway, stands a two-story house, a barn, and a large covered carport with a truck, a tractor, and what could be a mini bulldozer if I were to guess.

Ethan parks the motorcycle under the carport. "I haven't seen lights coming from this place in months."

"Oh. Did you ever visit the owner, Roman Novak?" I loosen my hold.

Cold air blows between my body and his, and I shiver.

"Yeah. Sometimes." His eyes skim the length of my legs, which are still hugging the sides of the bike.

The wind picks up and thick sheets of rain blanket the night.

"You said, you didn't live far from here." A gust chills my exposed skin, and my goose-pimpled flesh erupts with a new wave of goosebumps.

"I don't." He points toward a hill where a single bluish glow illuminates the night. "I live there—where the light is."

"Come on." He offers a hand and helps me climb off the seat. Once I'm free of the bike, Ethan stands.

"Hold this a minute." I shove my purse into his hands.

"Yes, ma'am." A grin tugs at the corners of his lips.

"Where are you?" I dig through each pocket. "I know you're here, somewhere."

"Are you sure you're expected? The house is dark."

"Uhm. Yeah." My focus remains on the backpack and the items within.

The butt of the handgun peeks out between the folds of the inner lining.

"Protection?" He clears his throat.

"Yep."

"Know how to use it?"

"Yeah. Point and squeeze."

He rubs the stubble on his chin. "What are you lookin' for?"

"Found it"—I extract my phone and uses it as flashlight—"now, to find . . ."

"Doesn't look like anybody's home."

"That's because there's no one else here but the two of us."

I shove a hand in the oversized side pocket and feel around.

The post of an earring jabs the tip of my finger, and rectangular pieces of mint bubble gum—free of the bonds of their plastic prison dispenser—roam free at the bottom of the compartment along with lent, pens, jewelry, and a few paperclips.

"Found them." I shake a set of keys. "Let's go."

I shoulder the purse and run out from under the carport.

"Wait up." A clash of thunder consumes his words.

Rain pelts my shoulders, face, and back, then trickles down my neck.

Flipping the collar of the jacket, I cover my ears, hoping to stop the flow of fluid drenching my blouse.

Square pavers offer a path through the torrential rain, but halfway to the front door, a stream of water swallows three of them, at least, by my estimation.

Once in the house, should I send him on his way or not?

Inviting him inside is the least I could do.

Plus, it's really raining now, and with the motorcycle . . .

He's a stranger, though.

It's not as if I really know anything about him other than he wears leather and what he drives. Hell, he could be an ax murder waiting for a chance to pounce.

Pounce. The word has so many different meanings: to jump on, swoop upon and seize, or a fine powder once used to prevent ink from spreading—often used for creating stenciled patterns.

Jeez. Get a grip already.

Of those phrases, the first of the three definitions, *jump on*, blankets my mind.

Hmm. Would it be so bad if he pounces? A grin tugs at my lips. *Could be fun from a research perspective.*

I always avoid the 'bad boy' type, though.

Annie, a woman who took care of me from the age of five to fifteen, and the only foster parent I considered a motherly figure worth trusting, used to point guys like Ethan out.

Now, you steer clear of a buck like that, she'd shake an aged finger in the air. *Them young'uns only want what's between your legs, girl. So, when they come a knockin' you send 'em packin'.*

That placement, which was one of the happiest in my life, had lasted ten years, two months, and twenty-seven days—a massive coronary ended that stent.

In front of a growing puddle of water that resembles a fast-moving stream, I come to a full stop.

Ethan, on the heels of my feet, bumps into me, sending me sliding ankle deep into the brown-colored fluid.

"What do you mean, there's no one else here?" He wraps an arm around my waist, keeping me on my feet. "Where's Roman?"

A flash of lightening streaks across the night sky, followed by a clash of thunder.

"He, uhm . . ." A howl fills the night, and I freeze in my tracks. I clutch his arm and stare into the blackness, searching. "What was that?"

The eerie sound echoes around me again, but this time, two more cries join in. One higher-pitched, and the other drawn out—like a tornado warning system—the unnerving clamor makes the fine hairs on my neck stand on end.

"You don't want to know." Ethan grabs me by the arm, and he half drags me toward the house. "We need to get inside. Now."

I follow him up the walkway and then take the stairs two at a time to keep up with his longer stride.

A deep growl rumbles in the darkness and a hulking, four-legged body, with two red, glowing eyes, slowly approaches.

Standing at the front door, my body trembles. "What the hell is that?" A shiver shakes me from head to toe. "A dog?"

I squint, hoping to focus on the distorted figure through the falling rain.

"Did Roman have a pet?" The keys slip between my wet fingers and clang against the wood planks. "A really big, fucking *Cujo* dog?"

Ethan scoops the keyring off the wooden platform and jams the house key into the lock.

Two more creatures, with the same hideous eyes, inch their way closer to the front door.

"Oh, God, there's more of them."

"S-a-d-i-e." The creature draws out my name. "Sadie. Sadie. Sadie."

When the steel door opens, Ethan yanks me inside. He slams it shut and engages the deadbolt.

Did that thing just talk?" My eyes widen.

He turns around and locks gazes with me, his expression unreadable. "Who the *fuck* are you?"

I step back, placing some distance me, the door, and Ethan. "I-I told you, Sadie Reed from San Antonio, Texas."

Looking away from his piercing stare, I examine my surroundings and basks in the warmth of the house, which is a welcome change from the chilly, wet air outside.

"Yeah. You said that already."

A large leather couch sits in the middle of the rectangular room with a chaise on one side and matching recliners on the other.

With the drapes open on the far wall, I feel exposed, naked to the prying eyes outside.

"What are those things?"

Making my way across the floor, I leave puddles of water in my wake.

"Why . . . how did it talk?"

I pull the curtains closed and then move into the next room bathed in moonlight, an office.

A streak of lightning flashes outside the window, illuminating the night.

Searching the front yard, I look for any movement or signs of life.

The frame of the sill sits level with my hip. Leaning close to the glass, I peer at the ground that's more than seven feet away.

Shadows dance in the darkness, but nothing living comes into view.

It wasn't real. I gulp a breath. *The wind's playing tricks on my mind.*

Standing on the tips of my toes, I grab the drapes and drag the two panels together.

The ping of shattering glass echoes through the house.

I pivot on the balls of my tennis shoes, which squeak on the hardwood floor, and I come face to face with a red, glowing set of eyes.

"H-how the *hell* did you get inside?"

The animal creeps closer, inch by inch. It's stalking me, closing the gap between me and it. And the closer the ominous orbs come; the larger the beast's overall mass appears.

Its ears tuck flat against its head. The dark hair on its back stands on end. A long snout with gleaming white fangs snarls.

It stands upright on two legs.

"What the fuck?" I gasp.

It's bipedal like a man.

"Run." Ethan grabs my arm.

He shoves me into the hall behind him, and I take off sprinting

"Find a place to hide." His body is all that stands between me and the approaching animal.

"What about you?"

"Do it. Now."

The creature extends a hand and digs talon-shaped

claws into the sheetrock. Advancing forward, he leaves four long slashes.

Ethan lunges forward, tackling the half-man, half-beast to the floor.

At the end of the hallway, I come to an arched opening, leading to a formal living room.

To my left, another animal, with red eyes, emerges from the shadows. It rises to full height and swipes at me.

"What the fuck?"

Another fur-covered creature perches on the sill of the broken window.

"Oh, God." I sidestep and race up the staircase. "They're everywhere."

At the top of the stairwell, I slide the purse from my shoulder. Hand shaking, I wrap my fingers around cold steel.

"Sadie . . . S-a-d-i-e," growls the beast. "Ready or not, here I come." The beast, now standing fully erect, takes the stairs two at a time.

Removing my hand from the purse, my fingers tremble. My grip on the handle of the weapon slips.

"Fuck." I hold the gun out in front of me. It's heavier now than when I shot it at the firing range with Matt and Dana.

My hands bob up and down, and my shaking fingers make it hard to slide the safety off. I wrap my index finger around the trigger.

"Stop. I don't want to shoot you." I lock eyes with the intruder standing in front of me. "Don't come any closer."

He squats, then springs forward.

A solid blow to my chest knocks me to the floor. Gasping for air, I scurry across the hardwood, putting some distance between me and the creature approaching.

The dog, man-beast thing approaches on two legs, stops, and then looms over me.

His breath, hot and rancid, makes me gag.

Now or never. The words echo in my head.

You got this. It's like practice—just without the walking, talking, rabid man-dog.

Two-handed, I level the barrel of the gun, keeping his chest between the sights like Matt had shown me.

"You shouldn't point a gun unless you intend to use it." The words come out in more of a growl than normal speech.

He lunges for me.

Gasping for breath, I pull the trigger.

The recoil of the blast forces my hands back.

A dead weight falls on top of me, making it hard to breathe, much less move. The mixed aroma of chalk and scorched paper burns the inside of my nose.

"Sadie." Ethan's voice carries through the house. "Where are you?"

I open my mouth to speak, but nothing comes out, not even a squeak.

Footsteps pound against the wooden stairs. A figure, with golden eyes, approaches.

I struggle to slide out from underneath the man or beast, who is lying motionless on top of me. Freeing the hand holding the gun, I take aim at the oncoming mass.

"Stay back." Squeezing the trigger once again, the gun goes off for a second time.

The intruder grunts and rolls to the side.

Before I can take aim again, a hand wraps around my wrist, forcing my arms above my head. And the gun is ripped from my grasp.

"No. Please," the words come out a jumbled mess.

"It's me," says Ethan, barely above a whisper.

"Ethan?"

A heavy weight topples off me, and I'm yanked to my feet. Strong arms draw me into a tender embrace.

"Oh, God." I peer at the motionless form on the floor.

My stomach lurches.

It's a man, not a beast.

"I killed him." A swimmy sensation rolls through my head. "Oh, God, I just killed someone."

My knees buckle, and the strange, dark world spins around me. The last thing I see, before my vision goes black, are golden-colored orbs—Ethan's eyes.

CHAPTER SIX

———————

Ethan Cotter

THE COPPERY, METALLIC SMELL of blood fills the air.

Three distinguishable scents linger. Two of them belong to the dead lycans: one on the living room floor with his throat slashed, and the other, upstairs with a hole in his chest. Both reek of the Kweo clan. And the third, a sweet, alluring aroma, belongs to Sadie, who has just passed out.

She's not human, but she's not lupine or lycan, either. So, what the *hell* is she, and why'd she have a gun? And why the *fuck* did the Kweo pack attack on hallowed ground?

I slide the safety on, then slip the weapon inside the waistband of my jeans. The metal cools my lower back.

Scooping her up, I cradle her in my arms and carry her down the stairs. In the living room, I lay her on the couch.

Blood. She reeks of blood.

Cupping her chin, I tilt her head, first to one side,

looking for the source of the metallic stench, and then to the other.

A small section of her hair, wet and slick, sticks to the left side of her head.

I sniff, and my inner beast tastes the metallic aroma—blood, a mixture of both hers and her attacker's.

Mine, my inner beast whispers in the recesses of my mind.

A tinge of pain stabs at my heart.

Did the Kweo mark her? The thought sends my beast to the edge of frenzy.

The superficial wound on her head doesn't contain the markings of a bite. But the smell of the lycan's blood is strong, *so where's it coming from?*

I slide a hand over the leather jacket and sniff.

Four distinct slash marks mar the garment splattered with blood, lycan blood.

Wrapping my fingers around the zipper, I pull it down, and the teeth come undone, exposing her chest.

Her breasts rise with each inhale. The tank top, hugging her body, is intact.

Lowering my head, I draw in a deep breath.

The leather jacket holds the largest concentration of lycan blood. Continuing my search, I don't pick up the scent anywhere else on her body except for her hair.

She stirs and her lids flutter. A soft cry passes her lips.

"Sadie." I caress the side of her face. "Open your eyes." Her skin is smooth, flawless.

Her almond-shaped eyes spring open, and big brown irises hold my gaze.

"Were you bitten?" I struggle to keep my inner beast under control. "Did he bite you?"

"Bite . . . what?" Sadie shakes her head then grimaces. "Oow . . . my head hurts."

Gingerly, she runs a hand through her hair. She brings her fingertips in front of her face, and her eyes widen.

"Is that blood? Am I bleeding?"

"Listen to me," I say, softly. "Focus. Were you bitten?"

"No. I don't think so." She sits, clutching the back of the couch for support.

I take hold of the collar of the jacket and push it off her shoulders.

"What are you doing?" She crosses her arms over her chest and pulls away.

"I'm not going to hurt you." I point to the slash marks on the front of the garment. "I just want to make sure you're not injured."

She slips her fingers through the gashes.

"That could've been me." She swallows hard.

Sucking in a ragged breath of air, she slides the jacket down the length of her frame.

Taking hold of her wrist, I examine first her right arm then left. Other than the early formation of a bruise, she's unmarked.

"I saw the blood and thought"—my eyes travel over her tank top, across her breasts, and pause on her narrow waist for several seconds—"he'd bitten you."

"I'm okay, I think."

I continue to follow the flare of her hips to her exposed thighs, searching for any signs of a wound. Other than a scrape or two and a few bruises, I don't see any other injuries.

She clears her throat. "What were they . . . those things?" A tremor shakes her body. "They weren't right. They were—"

"Beasts. Half-bloods."

"Half-bloods?" She pauses. "The one I shot—it was—he was dog-like then took human form. Who or what does that?"

"A lycan. They were all lycans—even the rogues outside."

"Like a werewolf?"

"Yes." I nod my head. "Can you stand?" I offer a hand.

"I don't understand. They're not real. Werewolves aren't real—they're stories told around a fire to keep kids from wandering too far from camp. Myths. Lore even."

"Most myths are born from unexplainable events." He offers a hand once again. "Can you stand?"

"I think so."

"We need to go. It isn't safe here."

She places the tips of her fingers on the palm of my hand. "Go where?"

Her eyes gloss over and fill with tears. She blinks several times to stem the flow.

Mine, my inner beast whispers from within. *Must protect.*

I coax her to her feet. "Up the hill to my place."

"I can't go out there." Fear exudes from her body like an intoxicating drug.

The fragrant aroma draws the attention of my beast. *Mine,* it whispers once more. *Must protect Sadie Reed.*

Drawing her into my arms, I press her lean frame against me. Her body fits perfectly against mine.

"And then?"

"You'll be safe there. Protected." I cradle her to my chest, stroking her back, offering her what comfort I can.

The faint scent of her arousal piques the interest of the alert wolf inside me.

It sucks in her scent. My inner wolf has wanted females before, but this time it's different. The beast desires to claim her, make her his own and in turn, mine.

A deep-seated hunger grows inside me, building layer by layer. In all my years, I've never felt such a strong attraction or connection before.

I release her but wrap an arm around her waist because the wolf inside me refuses to relinquish its hold.

"Wait." At the door, she pulls back, and her body stiffens. "What if they're out there, those things—those animals?"

"Lycan. They're called lycans." I open the door and then draw in a deep breath, testing the air.

All that lingers of the rogues and the Kweo pack members is a residual, fading stench.

"They're gone, for now. But they'll return. And when they come back, they'll be in hunt mode." I usher her out the door. "We don't want to be here when they return."

"How do you know they're gone?"

Her big brown eyes stare. There's an innocence reflected in them that pulls at me.

"Because I'd smell them." I walk her to the motorcycle and sit down. "Hop on."

She hesitates, and narrows her eyes. "If you can smell them, then why didn't you know they were here earlier before they attacked?"

"They used the rain to mask their scent, which is why I didn't pick up on them." I motion for her to sit on the seat behind me.

"Does that mean you're one of them?" A tremor shakes her body. "One of those things?"

"Lycan. No." I hold out a hand. "And I'm not part of that tribe. Besides, I'd never hurt you, Sadie Reed."

"And why's that?"

"Because my wolf would never allow it."

"Oh." Sadie hesitates then takes my hand.

She straddles the bike, leans forward, and then wraps her arms around my waist.

The wolf inside me relishes her touch. I've never experienced such a strong need or attraction like this before.

My wolf knows what it wants. And right now, it is single-minded in its pursuit. It wants more. It craves more. It desires to mark Sadie Reed.

CHAPTER SEVEN

Sadie Reed

THE FAMILIAR FEEL of his body under my fingertips, and his scent, offers a degree of comfort.

When those things, the lycans, attacked, he stayed with me, protected me even.

So, what exactly does that make him?

He said he wasn't like them, and that the ones who attacked, the werewolves, were from the Kweo clan.

What the hell does that even mean? And how many other clans are there?

A gust of humid, balmy air blasts against my face, blowing long locks loose from the twisted, messy bun on the back of my head.

My hair whips against my face, neck, arms and back. I hug Ethan's body, using him as a shield against the wind.

It's no longer raining, but my soaked clothes offer no protection.

A coldness creeps deep into my bones that I can't shake,

causing me to shiver. Tightening my hold on him, I absorb the warmth of his body.

He's hot, the thought dawns on me, *and not just easy on the eyes*. His body is like a burning inferno.

Ethan pulls out of the Novak Ranch driveway. He turns right on to the two-lane highway, travels a couple of miles, and then turns in to a private paved road, which leads up a steep incline.

At the top of the hill, under the light of the moon, a single-story home comes into view.

I glance into the dense wooded area, wondering what's out there. Shadows snake through the trees, grass, and shrubbery, and my hair stands on end.

Are they there, watching? I shudder.

A circular light, hanging from a pole, illuminates the front of the house which has a log cabin-like feel to it with a modern, contemporary look.

In the gravel driveway, a black, double-cabbed truck sits alone. Near a storage building, a covered trailer cinched-up tight sports a logo that reads Cotter Construction.

Ethan pulls up next to the F150 vehicle and parks.

Like prior, he waits for her to slide off the seat before deploying the kickstand.

"Come on." He gets off the bike.

Standing on shaky legs, I follow him up the winding path leading to the house.

In the distance, a mournful howl pierces the shadows of the night.

My body shakes from head to toe. Picking up the pace, I close the small gap between me and Ethan.

"Those things—"

I reach for his hand and lace my fingers with his.

He glances over a shoulder. "Don't be afraid. I won't let anything, or anyone hurt you. You'll be safe here."

The door to the house swings open.

A guy, a few inches taller than Ethan, wearing frayed jeans, an unbuttoned shirt, and boots, steps out. The muscles of his ripped abdomen ripple with each step he takes.

He sniffs the air. "Who is your *friend*, little brother?"

"Sadie Reed," says Ethan. "Meet my brother, Cole."

CHAPTER EIGHT

Ethan Cotter

COLE STANDS IN FRONT of the opened door, blocking the entrance.

"Are you just going to stand there, gawking?" I wrap an arm around Sadie's waist, drawing her closer to my frame. "Or get the *hell* out of the way?"

"After you." Stepping to the side, Cole offers a welcoming gesture, but it doesn't look natural. It seems forced.

I guide Sadie through the house, into the kitchen, and pull out a chair.

"Have a seat." I plop down in a chair next to her.

Cole makes his way into the room, shoulders back and brooding.

His eyes glance over at Sadie and then fall upon me.

"Where's Ma?"

"She picked up a shift, but you'd know that if you were home when you were supposed to be." Cole stops in the archway between the kitchen and living area. "Your food is in the fridge. She put in there, not me."

"Not hungry right now."

Sadie rubs her eyes, then hugs her arms to her body. Goosebumps cover her exposed arms.

"Do either of you know what happened at Novak's place tonight?" Cole yanks the towels on the stove handle off.

He hands one to Sadie, then tosses me the other one.

"The word coming down the pipeline is that an animal and an unknown assailant broke into the house."

"That's not what happened. There were—"

"Seems they had a bit of a party. Things got out of hand, and they wrecked the place."

"No. That's not accurate." Sadie towel-dries her hair. "That's not how it happened."

Cole's steely eyes land on me. "Anything I should know?"

"I, we didn't break in." Sadie's eyes widen. "We didn't."

"Then what would *you* call it?" Cole slides a chair out from under the table, spins it around, and then straddles the seat. He plants his hands flat on the table. His eyes, dark and menacing, reflect the wolf inside him.

"It's not considered burglary when people enter their home."

My beast picks up on the anger hovering around her scent. And if it can smell the aroma, so can my brother, which will garner the attention of his inner beast.

"Look." I set the towel on the table. "I don't know what the fuck you heard, but—"

"Think long and hard about your next words before you speak them, little brother." Cole grabs Sadie's purse and empties the contents.

"What the *hell* do you think you're doing?" Sadie stands and reaches across the table. She gathers the items of her spilled purse and shoves everything into the bag. "Your brother's an ass."

"Yeah. Tell me something I don't know."

"Where's the gun? I know it's here." Cole wraps a hand around her wrist. "What the *hell* are you because you're not lupine or lycan?" He sniffs the air. "And you're *damn* sure not human."

Rising, I pull the handgun from my waistband.

"Calm down. It's not what you think."

He takes the weapon from my hand, ejects the magazine and empties the chamber, disarming the gun and then sets it on top of the table.

"Not what I think?" Cole brings Sadie's hand to his face and sniffs once more. "I can smell the residual gunpowder on her skin."

"Hey, listen up"—I reach for my brother's arm but stop mid-motion—"we didn't start it."

"No?" A throaty growl reverberates deep in Cole's chest. "Then you want to tell me why you two killed lycans on hallowed ground?"

"Hallowed ground? What are you talking about?" Sadie struggles to release Cole's hold. "Those things attacked me. They all did. They were trying to kill me—us." Sadie's voice cracks, and her lower lip quivers. "They got in the house. They weren't right. Their eyes, they were red and—"

"Let her go. She speaks the truth, brother."

I place a hand on her shoulder, trying to reassure and comfort her.

"Explain. Now."

"When we arrived at the house, a Kweo pack was there." I hold the house keys, shaking them. "They moved into position to attack before the key was even in the lock. Once we were inside, they smashed a window to gain entry."

I toss the jacket at my brother.

Cole sniff the garment then spreads it out on the table.

"Wait. This is *yours*."

"No shit! You gave it to me last winter."

He examines the slashes, then smells the front once again. "Why is there lycan blood on it?"

Cole drops the jacket on the table and narrows his eyes.

"And why the hell does it smell like her?"

"Because Sadie was wearing it when attacked." I struggle to keep my wolf at bay.

"I can smell your blood on it." Cole drags Sadie from her seat. "Where did the Kweo mark you?"

"Mark me?" She yanks her arm free of his grasp. "What are you talking about?"

"Where were you bit?"

I step between Sadie and my brother.

"Back off. They didn't bite her. The blood you smell is from a superficial wound on her head she got when she fell. She's not marked. I checked."

Not yet, anyway but she will be if my wolf has anything to do with it.

"Sit." The single word echoes in the kitchen. "Both of you."

"It's okay." I motion for her to take a seat.

Cole examines the wound on Sadie's head. "You don't need stitches." He reaches for the towel she's holding, takes it from her hand, and then presses it to her head.

"Oow." She flinches. "That hurts."

"Hold it there. The bleeding has almost stopped." He turns to me. "Start talking."

"I thought it was the rogue, at first, the one mutilating cattle and other livestock, but there were too many of them."

"A chance meeting or planned attack?" Cole straddles the chair once more.

"Well, I don't think it was a coincidence if that's what you're asking. Fuck, no. The attack wasn't random. They were looking for something."

"Or someone." Cole stares Sadie down. From the look on his face, he's struggling to reigh in his wolf. "Who are you?"

"I don't have to take this shit." She rises, grabs her cell, and then huffs. "Fuck. That's just great."

Tears well in her eyes, and she tosses the device on top of the table.

"No fucking reception." She swipes at the tears running down her cheeks. "I hate this place—Kensington Cove."

"It's the storm." Taking hold of Sadie's hand, I coax her back to the table "The rain messes with the towers. You'll be able to call out when it stops."

I blot my face with the towel and then wipe off the excess water dripping from my hair.

"I shouldn't have come here." She slips on to the chair and cradles her head. "Fresh air. Fresh start." Her voice cracks. "He said it'd be good—"

"Who?" A need to know more eats at me.

"Doesn't matter now."

"How did the two of you meet?" Cole leans on the table, both elbows on the surface.

"Shit. My car." Sadie sinks back into her chair and holds my gaze. "It's on the road."

"Road?" I shake my head. "No. I'm pretty sure it's still in the ditch you drove it into." I grin, wolfishly.

"What the hell are you talking about?" Cole rises, grabs the towels, and hangs them.

"Sadie here was checking her phone, driving in the middle of the highway not far from Roman's place. She almost plowed over me."

"I did not. And I wasn't driving in the middle of the road." She sighs. "Okay. So, I may have swerved a bit, but I wouldn't have hit you."

"Interesting story." Cole rest a hip against the stove. "I'll have someone pick up your car in the morning." He pauses. "I'm making some coffee. Do either of you want some?" He grabs a filter out of the cabinet. "It's gonna to be a long night."

"Yes." Sadie nods. "Please."

A quick sniff of the air in the room confirms Cole's initial anger lingers but no longer climbs in intensity.

"Yeah. I could use some about now." I rise. "But I could also use a shower and some dry clothes."—I hold Sadie's gaze—"Unless you'd like to take one first."

Cole grabs three mugs from the cabinet and sets them on the counter.

"No. I'm good." Sadie shakes her head. "Wait. You're not going to leave me alone with him, are you?"

"You'll be fine." I walk to the far side of the kitchen and turn around. "Cole will be on his best behavior, right?"

Cole grumbles something unintelligible.

Sadie leaps from her chair.

"Sit down!" Cole's voice contains an air of authority not to be questioned. "We're not finished talking."

Without a peep, Sadie slides on the seat again.

"Have some coffee." Cole sets a steamy cup in front of her. "It's decaffeinated because you damn sure don't need any caffeine as wound up and jittery as you are." A slight grin flashes across his lips, but it's gone just as fast as it had first appeared.

Chuckling, I walk out of the kitchen. I know Cole well enough to know that Sadie's safe. And who knows, maybe he'll get more out of her—a story—one that I did get.

He's a real ass at times, but when shit goes down, I can count on him to cover my back.

Stepping into the bathroom, I shed my wet clothes and enter the shower. My hand hovers over the hot knob then drifts to the cold. As worked up as my inner wolf is, frigid water would be the better choice. But at this rate, I'm not even sure if a cold shower will be enough to douse the raging fire burning deep inside.

My wolf wants one thing, and one thing only. It wants her, Sadie Reed.

CHAPTER NINE

Sadie Reed

THE TENSION IN THE AIR is thick.

I wrap my hands around the mug and sip on the black coffee. It's bitter, and I scrunch my nose.

Cole sets a sugar container on the middle of the table.

"Do you use creamer?"

"Yeah." I nod and glance around the kitchen—a microwave with a broken handle hangs off the door.

I focus on pouring the sugar into my cup, anything to avoid Cole's probing stare.

"Here you go." He hands me a creamer carton, which I accept with a trembling hand. Using it quickly, I give it back. "Thanks."

Cole straddles the chair, again.

I can feel his searing, suspicious gaze burning into my head from across the table. It's as though he's searching, probing, trying to discover what secrets I now hide from him.

"How did you come to have keys to the Novak Ranch?"

"That's not any of your business," my voice cracks.

"Let's try that again." He leans into the table. "How'd you get the keys?"

I clear my throat and start over. "This morning, I learned an attorney had contacted social services a little over a week ago. The guy gave me some records and letters."

"And?" He pours creamer into his mug.

"One of the letters said something about me being named an heir to property."

"The Novak Estate?"

"Yeah." I wrap my hands around the mug, relishing the warmth. "Me, inheriting stuff, didn't compute. I thought it was a scam, so I just tossed the paperwork in the trash. But Dr. Gus talked to Social Services outside of the room."

"Who's Dr. Gus?" He spoones sugar into the steaming coffee.

"She's my principal, well, used to be, anyway."

"And the social worker?"

"Mrs. Berry, she's a real bitch. Works my case."

"We'll get back to what case she handles for you shortly." He takes a swig of coffee. "Continue."

"When they came back, I was told to pack my stuff because the Greene family was in jail."

"Who the hell are they?"

"The family Mrs. Berry had me living with."

"Why the fuck weren't you living with your parents—your family?"

"Because I don't have any." My lips turn down into a frown. "But then this morning, the attorney said I did."

Cole rubs his head. "Did what? Have family?"

"Uh, huh. The lawyer guy pulled out some documents, reports, and papers."

"You have a name?"

"For the attorney, yeah. Jared Lambett . . . Lambeth—"

"Lambert." Cole brings the mug to his lips but doesn't drink. "Jared Lambert."

"Sounds about right. Well, he claimed he'd been searching for me for the past several months."

Digging through my purse, I pull out Mr. Lambert's business card and hand it to Cole.

"He said I was the only living relative of his client."

"I know Jared, he and Roman go way back." He waves his hand, motioning for me to continue.

"I was skeptical, at first, and thought it really was a scam." I rub some warmth into my arms. "Even thought he was an old creeper trying to get close to me at first. I just didn't know why."

"Why do you say that?"

"Growing up in the foster care system has a way of making someone feel that way, you know, jaded and paranoid of strangers."

"Foster care?" He nearly spills his coffee. "What about your mother—father?"

"Never knew my birth mother—not even her name. Same with my father." I sigh. "Well, that is until Mr. Lambert showed up. My mother was Kim . . ." I pause. "Kimberly Novak, that's what he told me her name was."

"And your father?"

I shrug my shoulder. "Still don't know?" I unzip a large pocket inside her purse. "But Mr. Lambert gave me this." I hand him an envelope. He was supposed to meet me at a local burger joint today but got called into court."

"Is that so?" He examines the document. "What's in here?"

"My mother's death certificate, my birth records, and

the deed to Roman Novak's estate." I set more content on the table.

Cole scoops up the documents and reads over them.

"Uhm, Cole."

"Yeah." He glances up.

"What are ya'll? You and Ethan?"

"What'd he tell you?"

"Well, he said he wasn't lycan or Kweo when I asked." I brush hair out of my face. "He said he wasn't part of their tribe. What does that mean? What is he? What are you?"

He rubs his face, then holds my gaze. "Lupine." His expression softens. "We're lupines."

"What exactly does that mean?"

"Simply put, we're a type of skinwalker."

"And that means what?"

"Our kind can shift from human form to that of our inner beast." He slides the large envelope open and extracts the documents from inside. "We're shape shifters."

"You mean like the ones at the house?"

"No. A growl passes Cole's lips. "We're nothing like them."

"Why? What makes you different?"

"We're born this way—purebred."

I draw in a deep breath and hug my arms to my chest.

"Fuck. I feel as if this day sucked me into a warped, parallel version of the Twilight Zone."

I swallow a lump in my throat and struggle to maintain my composure. Extracting information from Ethan's brother is about as hard—and feels as dangerous—as pulling teeth from a gator.

"And how, exactly, are lupines different from lycans? I don't understand."

"Lupines are the direct decedents of ancient skin-walkers."

"People who can shift into wolves."

"Yes. And the lupine bloodline passes from parent to child, with each new generation birthed."

"What about the other ones, the lycans?"

His eyes remain glued a single file.

"Lycans are the product of a bitten host, human or other, which results in a hybrid called a werewolf."

A shiver runs up my spine. Even the warmth of the coffee isn't helping to dispel the chill in my bones.

"That's why you and Ethan asked if that thing had bitten me."

"Yeah." Cole flips through the paperwork. "Wait." His brows shoot up. "This says Roman's your maternal grandfather?"

She nods. "Well, yeah, since Kimberly, his daughter, was my mother. That'd make him my grandfather. Well, he was my grandfather."

"Was? You mean as in past tense?"

"Yes. He died three months ago." I shift some papers around and grab a death certificate. "Stage four liver cancer, I think. It's listed on this."

"And you knew nothing about your biological family until today?"

"No. The courts sealed the records, so I never had access to them."

"Shit." Cole slaps his hand on top of the table. "If you're a Novak then that changes everything."

"Why? What do you mean?"

"That'd make you part of one of the oldest bloodlines in Kensington Cove." He rubs his face. "You sure they said cancer?"

"Yeah. It's listed here." I point out the cause of death.

"Cancer, my ass." Cole stands and paces. "I have to talk to Keegan."

"Who is that?" I take a sip of coffee. "And why do you have to talk to him?"

"What'd I miss?" Ethan walks into the kitchen.

His bare feet slide across the floor without making a sound.

"What changes everything?" He's clad in only jeans. His wet hair glistens under the track lighting. "And what does Keegan have to do with anything?"

"Ask your new girlfriend," Cole growls under his breath. "Neither of you leave this house. I have to go." He holds up the documents. "Can I take these with me? I'll bring them back."

"Sure. I guess so." I place my elbows on the table and rest my chin on my hands.

"You haven't told me what Keegan has to do with this." Ethan walks up beside his brother.

Cole swallows the coffee left in his mug, places it in the sink, and then heads toward the living room.

"I'll let Sadie explain who her family is, or was," Cole calls out over his shoulder. "But right now, it's imperative I talk to Keegan."

Ethan grabs a cup of hot coffee, then turns around to face the table.

"So? Talk to me."

My eyes trail up the faded jeans hanging off his hips. Rock hard abdominal muscles, with a defined six-pack, fill my vision.

The memory of how those muscles felt under my fingertips when I held on to him floods my mind.

Warmth spreads through my body, generating intense heat between my legs.

Ethan draws in a deep breath, then grins. "Mmm. See something enticing."

"Wait. Did you just sniff the air?"

"I did." He licks his lips. "Wanna know what my inner beast smells?"

"No, thanks." My mouth waters, and I gulp a sip of coffee.

"You sure?"

I nod then squeezes my thighs together, willing all thoughts of bare skin rubbing against each other—moving as one—in a passionate embrace, to dissipate.

Ethan clears his throat not once but twice. It's as if he can read my mind.

Finally, I gaze up. My eyes lock with his.

An intense heat warms my cheeks. "I uhm . . ."

"Can I get you anything?" A wolfish grin spreads across his face. "Coffee. Tea—"

"No. No, thanks." My comment sounds more like little squeaks than words.

"Are you sure that you don't *want* anything else?" His intense, probing eyes drink in my form.

I nod then shake my head once more, unable to speak.

A wolfish smile rolls across his lips.

"How about that shower?" His voice is husky and thick.

"Sure. Okay," I say, barely above a whisper.

At this point, some time alone in a bathroom—away from him, far, far away from him—sounds like an excellent idea.

CHAPTER TEN

Ethan Cotter

"TOWELS ARE IN THERE." I point at the linen closet in the far left of the room. "And you'll find shampoo, conditioner, and soap in the shower."

I linger in the open doorway. The wolf inside me inhales her arousal, which kicks up my libido another few notches.

"Can I get you anything else?"

"No." She shakes her head.

"I left a T-shirt and a pair of boxers on the counter. It's all I have. When you're done, I'll show you where the washing machine is."

"Okay. Thanks." She closes the door, and the lock engages.

I loiter, waiting, and lean against the door, listening. Her footsteps softly drum against the floor.

The spray of the shower mutes her movements, so that's

my cue. I make my way into the living room and plop on the couch.

Lying back, eyes closed. Images of Sadie's long legs fill my mind.

"Mmm." The wolf inside me licks its lips.

He'd like nothing better than to have those legs wrapped around him or spread eagle across a bed, displaying the alluring flower between her luscious thighs.

My dick pulses. It begs to plunge inside the velvety warmth she has to offer.

"Fuck. What the hell's wrong with me?"

I grab the remote and switch on the television. A classic movie marathon list flashes on the screen.

After flipping through a few of the other channels, I decide on the old 1931 *Frankenstein* movie with Colin Clive, Mae Clarke, and Boris Karloff.

The water in the bathroom shuts off.

My ears perk, and my body tenses with anticipation.

I lower the volume on the television, which isn't necessary. The fine-tuned hearing of my inner wolf could easily hear a pin drop in the house even with every television, radio, and appliance running.

The patter of bare feet putters against the hardwood floor. The pace slows the closer the steps come to the living room.

Even with my eyes closed, I can feel her gaze roaming over my body.

A combination of soap, shampoo, and her scent wafts in the air. The longer she stares, the stronger her lust grows.

The wolf inside me growls. It wants to act, pull her into his arms and take her. But I know I mustn't let him move too fast, or *we* could end up frightening her.

"Uhm . . . Ethan." Her voice travels through the living room. "Where's the laundry room?"

I open my eyes, scoot to the edge of the couch, and feast on her form.

"Don't get up." There's a nervous edge to her voice. "Just point me in the right direction. I can handle washing my stuff."

She walks into the room and glances at the television.

"I didn't peg you as an old movie buff. At least, not monster ones, anyway."

"Really? So, what'd you *peg* me for?" I lick my lips, hoping there isn't any drool. *"The Hounds of Baskerville or A Werewolf in London?"*

"I didn't mean to—"

A rose-tinted blush colors her cheeks and neck.

"Just messing with you." I lean against the back of the couch. "I don't mind the classics."

The gray T-shirt she's wearing hangs about mid-thigh. A hint of the blue cotton boxers peeks out from underneath the hem of the shirt.

"Uhm. The laundry?"

"Oh, yeah. It's off to the right of the kitchen." I point in the general direction. "You can't miss it."

She walks in front of me, and the sway of her hips draws my undivided attention, at least, until she exits my view.

Eyes closed again. I listen to her light steps patter on the hardwood floor. Once on the granite tile, her soles slap against the surface.

The click of the machine lets me know she's preparing to wash a load.

Lying on the couch, I focus on the sounds in the house: the hum of the refrigerator, water swooshing in the washing machine, and her pacing back and forth on the tile.

Five minutes pass, and she hasn't returned.

A smile stretches across my face. Her nervous energy has her adrenaline pumping.

Rising, I stretch my arms overhead, then prowl through the kitchen and then into the laundry room, stalking my prey.

Perched in the entrance, appreciating the view of her well-toned legs, drool dribbles from the corners of my lips. I swipe it with the back of a hand.

Standing on the tips of her toes, she reaches across the folding counter to the middle open shelf.

Her fingertips brush the corner of the dryer softener box, pushing it just out of reach. Lifting a leg, she climbs on to the edge of the counter, and then retrieves a few sheets.

When she pivots around, her eyes widen.

"Jeez. Make some noise or something next time. I didn't hear you."

"Find everything okay?" I enter the ten by ten room.

She nods and backs against the counter across from the upright washer.

"You live alone?" She fidgets with the hem of the shirt she's wearing. "I mean is it only you, your mother, and brother?"

"Why?" Ethan approaches. "You interested?"

"J-just curious." The erratic thumps of her heart increase in tempo. "Seems really clean for two guys in a house."

"As opposed to what? Your backseat?"

"Hey." She nudges me. "Cut me some slack, I'm moving."

"Okay. Fine." A chuckle passes my lips. "And yeah . . ."

"Yeah what?"

"Sorry to disappoint you, but it's just the three of us." I

lean against the wall next to her. "I guess you can say, my brother and I are house-trained. Oh, and no, I don't have girlfriend unless you'd like to fill that spot."

A smile dances across her lips, crinkling the corners of her eyes.

"Oow." She squeezes her lids shut, then traces the base of her cheekbone and temple with the tips of her fingers.

The smidgeon of a bruise surfacing darkens the contours of her face.

Anger feeds the belly of the beast within me. It would like nothing more than to hunt the abominations who inflicted the pain.

"And your father." Her eyes, big and full of curious wonder, hold my gaze.

"He died a few months back. Hunting accident."

"I'm sorry."

Standing in front of her, I cup her chin, tipping her head back. "Hurting?"

"Yeah, a bit." Each time her lids flutter, her thick, full lashes fan out, reminding me of the delicate wings of a butterfly. "But it's not bad."

"How about you"—I hold her gaze—"single or taken?"

"Why do you ask?" The corners of her mouth twitch, making the dimples in her cheeks wink. "You interested?" She tosses my words back with a smooth finesse.

I wait for a response, knowing full well, she's alone because if she had a boyfriend or lover, I would smell him on her. And her sweet, alluring essence is the only aroma to emanate from her shapely form.

"Oh, yes, Sadie Reed." I press a hand against the wall next to her head. "I'm definitely interested." Closing the distance between her body and mine, I press my frame against hers. "How about you?"

"I, uhm." She chews on the inside of her lip.

The enthralling scent of her increasing arousal puts my inner beast on heightened alert.

My wolf focuses on her physical reaction: dilation of pupils; plump, rose-colored lips; a lustful blush that brings color to her smooth flesh.

I lean next to her ear, taking in the rapid beats of her heart. "Do I make you nervous?"

"Nope." The word comes out as a soft squeak.

She ducks under my arm, trying to slide by.

Testing the air, not a trace of fear wafts, so I press on.

Placing my hands on each side of the counter, I block her exit.

"Are you sure?" A grin washes across my face. "And before you respond, just know, my wolf can read you like an open book."

"Is that a fact?" A single brow arches, and a defiant glint twinkles in her eyes.

"Yeah. It is."

"So, tell me what you *think* you know."

"Your heart races every time we're in close contact."

I caress the side of her face with a thumb, stopping at the edge of her mouth—the mouth I long to taste.

"Desire causes your lips to flush, your body to blush, and your pupils to dilate." I sniff the air, breathing in her growing arousal. "Shall I continue?"

"Okay. Fine." She swallows hard. "Maybe you make me a little bit nervous."

"Only a little?"

Lowering my head, I press my lips to the curve of her cheekbone. "—sure about that?"

My breath flutters over her flushed skin, compelling her to blush once more.

"Uhm. Wait." She presses her palms against my chest. "What other things are you talking about?"

She squirms but doesn't leave.

"I can smell you. Your arousal lingers in the surrounding air. It's sweet, appetizing."

Leaving a trail of kisses across the side of her face, I nudge closer to her mouth. An inch from her lips, I pause. Her arousal is even stronger than before.

Got you. The wolf inside me grins.

"I want you." Slowly, I claim her mouth, teasing, coaxing her to open to me. As soon as her lips part, I plunge my tongue into the soft, warm recesses of her mouth.

She's sweet and yielding.

Without breaking eye contact, I slide a hand to her hip, and then caresses her thigh. The contact makes her quiver.

She sucks in a quick breath, and her lids spring open. Her eyes, now dreamy and heavy-laden with desire, hold my gaze.

Slipping a hand inside the hem of the boxers she's wearing, I trace the curve of her thigh.

"Uhm . . ." Her heart thumps in her chest, keeping a fast cadence.

"All you have to do is tell me *no* if you don't want me to continue." I pause my explorative quest.

"I don't do this." Her eyes widen. "You know, move this fast." A nervous energy swirls around her. "I'm not—"

"Do you want me to stop?" I reel in the wolf's libido and focus on reading the unspoken clues her body freely provides.

Silence thickens the air.

The flush of her skin and an increase in saliva, along with her plump lips and lust-filled dreamy eyes, beacons me on; however, her hesitation and rising anxiety sends a mixed message—one of uncertainty.

My wolf and I yearn to hold her, taste her, have her—to claim her, something I've never entertained with any female until now. But I don't want to move faster than she's willing or ready to go.

"Talk to me." I nuzzle her neck. "Tell me what you want."

"I, uhm"—she draws in a slow, steady breath—"I like you, a lot, actually, which is odd since we just met."

"The feeling is mutual."

"But I don't know you?"

"What would you like to know?"

She casts her gaze to the floor, avoiding my eyes.

"Can you change?" Her words come out barely above a whisper. "You know like those things, the lycans?"

"Yes. I can take the form of a half-man, half-beast, but my kind, lupines, also shift into grey wolves."

"Is that what I heard howling back at the car? A wolf, or was it one of them—a lycan?"

"Could've been either one." I slide a hand through my hair, combing rogue strands out of my face.

A yawn rolls across her lips, accentuating the tired lines and dark circles under her eyes.

"Let's go sit." I check the timer on the machine. "Can't toss your stuff in the dryer for another twenty-five minutes, anyway."

CHAPTER ELEVEN

Sadie Reed

EYES HEAVY, I drift on the strings of sleep. A steady beat thumps in my ear, pulling me closer to a dream world.

An image of Ethan's face materializes in my mind's eye. Looking in his gaze, I've never known such comfort or contentment. Since I first met him, I've felt a connection, a bond growing between me and him, which only grew stronger in the house when he offered his protection.

A sensation of falling makes my body jerk, and my eyes spring open.

"You okay?" He brushes some stray hairs out of my face.

"Yeah." I nod and do a mini stretch. "I must've dozed off."

Now alert, the source of the steady cadence in my ear—his heartbeat—makes my body warm with a full-on flush.

"Sorry." Lifting my head from his chest, I reposition my upper body and sit erect.

Moisture coats my lips. *Oh, God, did I drool on him?* A

renewed heat warms my cheeks.

An inspection of his shirt reveals only the dry material of the fabric.

"How long was I out?" I cover a yawn with the back of a hand.

He glances at the watch on his wrist. "About four hours."

"My clothes." I leap from the couch.

"Already dry." He points to a folded stack of garments.

My bra sits on top of the display, offering a glimpse at the elastic band outlining the cup.

Great. Just what I needed—a guy fondling and folding my undies.

Ethan shifts on the couch and reaches for my arm.

His grip, firm but gentle, makes me acutely aware of just how much hotter his skin feels against mine.

"Can I ask you a question?"

"Sure." He coaxes me on to the cushion next to him. "Ask away."

"Your body temperature, it's hotter, right?"

"Not too much higher, but yeah. It runs around 99.5 to 100."

"What about your heartbeat?" I draw my legs on to the couch under me and slip my toes between the cushions. "Faster or slower?"

He takes hold of my wrist and places my palm inside his shirt.

"Faster. But I can consciously slow the beat, especially during transformation."

"Cole, too?"

"Yes." The steady beat of his heart reduces speed and intensity.

"Does it hurt when you change?"

"No. Not really."

His eyes trail to the left, indicating he's thinking or recalling a memory—or so my biology teacher had said last week.

"I can feel it, but nah, it's not painful."

"Do you stay you"—I lock gazes with him—"when you change?"

"Of course. It's not as if I shift into a different person."

"No. That's not what I mean." I skim the tips of my fingers along the curve of his neck and follow the line of his jaw. "Do you retain your humanity?" The fine stubbles tickles. "Do you remember who you are now and your thoughts?"

"Yes. Transformation doesn't alter the person I am, it only changes the form I take." He sniffs the air. "But it does heighten the senses of my inner beast."

"Senses?"

"Namely smell and sight."

"And in this form?" I touch the messy strands of hair covering his left temple. They slide like silk through my fingertips. "Are they heightened?"

I'm drawn to the bow of his lips and left wondering what a kiss would feel like.

"More than those of a human."

"Earlier, you stated you could smell me—my arousal." A warmth heats my cheeks.

"I did." His tongue skims across his lower lip.

"So, what do I taste like?" I lean in and he meets me halfway.

"I'll let you know."

His lips, warm, firm, and skilled, claim my mouth. He toys with my lower lip, nipping on it, and then his tongue dances around mine.

"God," Ethan whispers in my ear. "What are you doing to me? Since I met you, you're all I think about." He reclaims my lips.

I wrap my arms around his neck, lacing my fingers through his hair.

His body stiffens, and he springs to his feet, breaking contact.

I place a hand against my tingling lips. "What's wrong?"

He holds a finger to his lips. "Shh."

The door handle jiggles.

A bone-chilling howl pierces the night.

"What the hell was that?" I scuttle off the couch. "Is it one of those things?"

The front door swings open, and a gust of wind chills the air.

A man with piercing, amber-colored glowing eyes looms in the doorway. "Where is she?"

Ethan steps in front of me. "What's going on, Keegan?"

"Is he wolfing out?" *Okay, Keegan is a bit intimidating. Well, a whole lot intimidating.*

More howls funnel in from outside.

Keegan enters, followed by Cole, who shuts the door.

"The clans have gathered as you can hear." Keegan approaches. His eyes, a deep cobalt blue now, offer a sharp contrast against his olive complexion. "They want the girl."

Blue-black hair hangs around his face. His features, sharp and contoured, exudes masculinity with an underline predatory sense.

Fear bubbles inside me, making the muscles in the pit of my stomach twist. "I don't understand."

I've read countless books and watched enough movies about werewolves and other creatures to know, at this moment, Keegan's the hunter, so that makes me the prey.

Hell, I've seen my fair share of National Geographic and know what an alpha member of a pack looks like. I might not know how wolf clans work, but I sure as hell know how wild dogs fight for supremacy in the wild.

There's pecking order, and from what I can see, Keegan sits on top of it.

"W-why me?"

Is this situation any different than out in the wild? Are lupines?

"Because you're Kindred," replies Keegan.

"What the *hell* is that?" The word slams into my mind a few times but the meaning remains elusive.

"Come here." Keegan extends an open hand.

Is he addressing me like a dog? What the fuck?

"Uhm. Nope." I shake my head. "Thanks for the offer, but I'm good over here."

"That's not a request"—Keegan's words utter a tone of warning—"it's an order."

Keegan sniffs the air. His eyes narrow, and he ushers a deep, throaty growl.

He turns dark eyes upon Ethan. "What the *fuck* have you done now?"

I take a few steps back, then stumble.

The bathroom comes to mind. *But can I reach it before he catches up with me?*

Keegan covers the gap between me and him and then shoves Ethan out of the way.

A new wave of terror creeps the length of my spine. I pivot on the balls of my feet. My soles smack the cold tile. First one step then another.

"Not so fast."

Grabbing hold of the T-shirt I'm wearing, he stops me dead in my tracks, and then drags me to his muscular frame.

"Did he stake a claim to you?" His hot, minty breath blows across the side of my face.

"W-what? Please." Fear wells deep inside my belly. "I don't understand."

"Did he bite you?" Keegan turns to Ethan. "I can smell you on her along with the lingering aftermath of lust. So, did you mark her?"

"No." Ethan shakes his head. "I didn't because she doesn't understand what it means. But I *do* stake a verbal claim to her now."

"Fuck," Keegan says under his breath. "Son-of-a-bitch. Do you know what you've done? What you've both done: you by coming here"—his eyes cut deep into my soul—"and him for latching on like a suckling whelp?"

"Where does this leave us?" asks Cole. "Already, the heads of the other clans are talking outside the house."

"What does that even mean?" Red glowing eyes wash through my mind, and I shiver. "Why me?"

"They're demanding her release." Cole stays standing in the entry.

"Wait." Fear rips through me. "Are you turning me over to them"—I point to the mob outside the window—"or to those beasts from Roman's house?"

Keegan growls, again. "You may be young and ignorant to our ways, to our brethren, but that doesn't mean you're exempt." He drags me closer to the door. "And let's not forget, you and Ethan killed two Kweo scouts."

"What are you talking about? What's a Kindred?" I struggle against his hold, trying to free myself. "And we were protecting ourselves."

"You don't know what a Kindred is?" Cole rises to full height, towering over me. "You're *fuckin'* kidding, right?"

"No," I say to Cole. "I'm not. I've no idea what you're

talking about."

"You're half lupine and half witch—an elemental—a female at that, which is rare. Therefore, you're what our brethren calls Kindred." Keegan wraps a hand around my wrist. "And as for the lycans you two killed—"

Half lupine, half witch, the thought swirls around. *Which one comes from my grandfather?*

"But I was defending myself." My gaze travels from Cole to Keegan. "We both were."

"Doesn't matter." Keegan tightens his hold. "You spilled blood on hallowed ground. Therefore, law requires justice."

"But that glowing-eyed bastard attacked me first, and the other went after Ethan. If I hadn't shot him, he would've killed me." I struggle to free his hold. "And who are you to sit as judge and executioner?"

"The council will decide your fate, not me."

"Let go." I grip his fingers with mine and try to pry them off. "I should've never come to this shit hole." Tears stream down my cheeks.

Ethan growls and steps forward.

"Don't." Cole shoves his brother back.

"Stay put, Ethan. You've done enough." Keegan points an accusing finger at him. "I'll deal with you later."

Keegan drags to me a window and pulls the curtains all the way back.

"Stop it." I stumble, then regain my footing.

"Do you see those men?" He shoves me closer to the windowpane.

"Yes." I fight to remain in control of my emotions, which right now, have me on a rollercoaster ride I can't seem to stop.

"They're here because of you." Keegan motions to the window.

"But I'm nobody."

"Nobody? You. Are. Kindred." Keegan pauses, allowing silence to suffocate the breathable air. "Because of you, before morning, there'll be more of them. Already, the Shoshone, Black Foot, Lakota, and Kweo have each staked their claim."

"What? To me?" *It makes no sense.* "I'm a person, not livestock."

Outside, droves of men and a few women dot the twilight landscape.

"No. You are Kindred."

Keegan loosens his hold and leans closer to the window. The irises of his eyes take on a reddish-amber glow once again.

Is he using wolf-a-vision? The thought tumbles around.

"What are you doing?" I stare out into the darkness. "What do you see?"

Bet it's better than night vision goggles. Oh, my God. What the fuck is wrong with me. Focus already.

"Son-of-a-bitch." Keegan shakes his head, then sighs. "*Fuck.*"

"What?" I search the darkness again, but my eyes only pick up on masses moving in the shadows.

Cole approaches the sill. "What's wrong?"

"The Formilia coven has arrived, which means other Wiccans aren't far behind." Keegan focuses on movement in the yard.

"Wiccans?" I strain my eyes to gain a better view. *Wish I had souped up eyes.* "Hold up. Do you mean witches?"

"Yes." Keegan's response is short and clipped.

Keegan's and Cole's eyes both glow a golden, coppery color, and the slits of their pupils look more canine than human.

"When you and Ethan killed the lycans from the Kweo clan, it brought discord to the doorstep of my kin, the Shoshone clan."

"I didn't mean to cause trouble." The words pass my trembling lips. "I didn't mean—if I could take back last night, I would. But I can't. So, what will happen to me—to us?"

"Now that it's known you're Kindred"—Keegan's words soften in tone—"your presence facilitates war."

"I didn't ask for that. I just wanted to come home—to my grandfather's place. Maybe even learn about him."

"None of that matters now."

"Maybe not to you, but it does to me." I scrunch my brows together, thinking. *Was my mother a wolf or a witch?*

Keegan releases me.

"As the alpha, the leader of my tribe, I'm being called out to release you to the chair heads of the Council of the Clans, to which I'm a member of, a head member at that."

I rub the red, angry flesh of my wrist.

Cole stands, arms crossed over his chest. "You've brought witches and warlocks to my soil—those from the Formilia coven.

"That means only one thing." Keegan turns his gaze on Cole.

"What now?" Ethan makes a move to approach.

"The Order of the Covens' Creed isn't far behind." Cole intercepts Ethan. "Sit your ass down."

"You can't turn her over to the Council of the Clans or to the Order." Ethan stands toe to toe with his brother.

"What if I don't want to go?" I slide past Keegan.

"Like you said"—Ethan rips free of Cole's hold—"she's an innocent in all this."

Keegan steps in front of me, reclaiming his hold on my

wrist and keeping his body as a barrier between me and Ethan.

"Do as your brother ordered." Keegan points to the couch. "Sit. Your. Ass. Down."

"Come on." Ethan stands his ground. "She didn't even know she was Kindred."

Keegan grabs Ethan by the neck with one hand, and then shoves him against the wall, all without relinquishing his hold on me.

"The laws are clear." He lifts Ethan's feet off the floor. "I'm to turn her over to the proper authorities because our clan doesn't have an explicit claim to her."

"Wait. What was my grandfather, Roman?" I twist my arm back and forth, trying to loosen Keegan's iron grip. "A witch or shifter like you?"

"Lupine." Keegan breaths the single word.

"What clan was he from?" I struggle to stay in control of my emotions.

"Shoshone." Keegan shakes Ethan. "Stop moving, whelp." He turns his attention back to me. "He was alpha before he named me."

Keegan releases Ethan, who crashes to the floor, coughing and gasping for air.

"Stay down." Keegan's words come out as a growl with a primal undertone.

"Then doesn't that make me part of the Shoshone clan by birth? Part of *your* kin?"

"No. Because you are Kindred," says Keegan, "And as a Kindred, you're born without a clan, which is why they sent you away."

A rap at the door makes me jump. "Don't give me to them. Please." My eyes fill with tears. "Ethan, do something."

Ethan, still coughing, rises. He takes two steps.

"Can't let you do that, little brother." Cole grabs Ethan, stopping him dead in his tracks.

The door swings open, revealing a woman with red hair and skin void of color.

"I am Agartha MacLauchlan, high priestess of the Formilia coven and the head of the Order of the Covens' Creed. I demand a word with the Kindred female, Sadie Reed, and an audience with Keegan and the Cotter whelps."

"No," Sadie's voice quivers. "I don't want to go. Please."

Ethan lunges forward, ripping free of Cole's hold. "Sadie."

Cole wrestles Ethan to the ground, restraining him. "Stay down."

Keegan holds out a hand and motions to Cole. "Release him." He glares at Ethan. "Control your wolf, or I will take you down." Turning around to face the floating woman, he demands, "Why are you here, witch? I didn't invite you into the home of my kin, my brethren."

Agartha shuts the door. "Send the others to another room, and let us talk, you and me."

"I'm not going anywhere." Ethan rubs his neck and coughs. "This is my house."

I place a hand on Ethan's shoulder. He wraps an arm around my waist, leaning against me for added support.

Agartha raises a brow. "Very well." She looks between me and Ethan before turning her attention to Keegan. "What I say now, must never leave these walls." She pauses. "I'm here on behalf of the Kindred, whom is of blood relation."

"Relation? How?" Keegan squares his shoulders. "Explain."

"I'm the girl's paternal grandmother, which you would be wise not to repeat." Agartha holds up a hand to silence the room.

"Zachary?" The name flows from Keegan's lips.

"No. My illegitimate son, Augustus, a high septon of the order, sired her."

"That breaks not one but several laws of the ancient Wiccan and Lupine treaty." A low-tone growl etches Keegan's words.

"Yes. And for these crimes, the septons executed him—with extreme prejudice." Her face remains emotionless. "For sixteen years, I upheld a secret truce between myself and one of your kin.

"Roman Novak." Keegan holds her gaze.

"It was his daughter, Kimberly, who carried the half lupine and half Wiccan offspring. Sadly, the mother died giving birth to the Kindred, so she never got to go to trial to plead her case on behalf of the child." She draws in a deep breath.

"I don't understand." A dizzy haze clouds my vision. "If I had a family, why was I sent away? He didn't want me? You didn't—" Tears well in my eyes.

"It wasn't a matter of want but survival." She floats closer. "Roman and I swore an allegiance to protect you, the infant, which we did by binding your powers right after birth.

"Binded? What's that?" Confusion creases the inner folds of my thoughts. "And why?"

"To keep you hidden and safe. And it worked, that is until Roman's recent death." She walks over to the couch and sits down. "Come. Join me. All of you."

"No." Keegan opens his stance, then crosses his arms over his chest. "I will stand."

Cole takes a seat in the recliner, keeping both the widow and the door in full view.

"Come, child. I will not harm you." Agartha motions to me. "Keegan, it is time for you and me to come to terms and agree upon a plan between clan and coven because turning the Kindred, my granddaughter, over, isn't a viable option."

I sit on the edge of the chaise next to Ethan.

"We should hear her out." I take in the features of the pale-faced woman, searching for any resemblance no matter how slight. "W-were you who I was supposed to meet—later at the house?"

"Yes, child." A sadness washes over her face. "You arrived alone and vulnerable, a regret I cannot change; however, with help, I can now ensure your safety."

"Tell me what you need. What you ask of me?" Keegan shifts weight from one foot to the other. He resembles a caged animal reluctant to stay in one place.

"Continue protecting her. She is special. We all know this. And once her abilities surface—"

"Abilities? There's nothing special about me. I'm as plain as they come."

"No, dear." A smile dances across Agartha's lips. "Your powers will surface now that you're no longer cloaked. Both clan and covens, alike, will seek to exploit you and your gifts." A touch of sorrow flashes across her eyes then vanishes as quickly as it appeared. "A predicament your grandfather and I feared most."

"What would you have my clan do—have me do?" An unreadable mask covers Keegan's face.

A wolf like grin tips the corners of her lips.

"Accept her into your clan. Claim or mark her as one of your own. That is what Roman would have done."

"By asking this, you're forcing me to go to battle with

both my brethren and Wiccans." Keegan shakes his head. "A path I cannot take."

"I know what I ask of you," she says. "But I also know lupines, lycans, and Wiccans both fear and respect you. Some will oppose you, but most will offer loyal support—whether they agree or not—because of the influential pull you have in all communities. Keep in mind, neither side wants to face war, again."

"What do you mean again?" *Wouldn't people know if supernaturals had been at war?*

"Even if I agreed to go along with your plan, the Kindred must submit, willingly, to being marked, to being claimed," says Keegan. "And she is not yet at the age of consent. Who would offer approval on her behalf? You?"

"Yes. As Wiccan and head of the Order, it's well within my rights." She clears her throat, then smooths her hair back with a single wave of her hand. "And there'd be no need to reveal the blood connection between Sadie and myself. No one must ever find out who sired her."

"What does that mean?" The information swirls around in my head.

I try to make sense of it all, but the connections float out of reach.

"Simply put, a Shoshone clan member leaves his mark on you.

"Meaning what, exactly?" My temples throb, and I furrow my brows.

"Claim you as a mate." Agartha sits erect, shoulders back.

She makes me think of the nuns at the church who took care of me until the age of five—those were days I wish I could forget sometimes.

Keegan approaches and sits on the arm of the couch. "Or mark you as a potential mate similar to an engagement."

"What happens?" I peer at Ethan. "What would *you* do?"

"If I were to claim you outright? I suppose during coupling, I would sink a canine tooth into your willing flesh." Ethan licks his lips. "And my saliva would run into your blood, making you mine."

"Or he could mark you with a single bite without sexual contact, which is more appropriate at her age and Ethan's." Keegan glances over a shoulder out the window. "More are converging outside, Wiccan and lupine alike."

"Wait. You want to *bite* me?" Memories of Ethan teasing me, saying he wouldn't bite unless I wanted him to, swirls around in my head.

"Yes." Ethan brushes his hair back and out of his face.

"What the fuck?" I leap from the couch. "That's why you said what you did, isn't it?"

Ethan nods. "When I said it the first time, I was joking. But the second time, the wolf in me wanted you. He had hoped to mark you, to claim you in time."

"How many others have you marked or still have your mark? *Hell.* How many females have you *all* staked a claim to?"

"You have this all wrong." Keegan holds his arms in the air, motioning for me to calm down.

"Don't try to shut me up." Anger seethes in my belly, growing in intensity.

"I've been with many women over the span of my life"— Keegan rubs his chin—"but I've never left my mark or claimed any of them as a mate."

"Span of your life? What the hell does that mean?" I draw in a calming breath through my nose, not really sure I want to know the answer. "On second thought, don't respond. I've had all the information I can process for one day." I turn and glare at Cole. "And what about you?"

"Don't look at me." Cole shakes his head. "I'm not ready to settle down. And I'm sure as hell not looking for a mate to fuck for eternity."

"What?" I pace back and forth.

Agartha grins. "Wolves mate for life, Sadie. When they stake a claim, they're monogamous and faithful to that person, forever."

Standing, my grandmother smooths the flowing layers of her skirt.

"However, there are options. You and Ethan share a strong attraction, even now, it's palpable in the room." She shifts her gaze to Keegan then to Cole. "Am I correct?"

"Yeah." Cole rubs the stubble on his face. "It's been that way since she first stepped foot inside. The scent is stronger now."

"What's that supposed to mean?" My cheeks heat up.

Flashes of me and Ethan in the laundry room roll through my thoughts.

"Hear me out." Agartha takes me by the hand, then sits once more. "Join me." She pats the couch cushion next to her.

I slip on to the sofa. *Is she a cookie making grandmother or something else entirely?*

"Ethan doesn't have to claim you outright." She pauses. "He could mark you as Keegan had suggested earlier, which signifies a waiting period, engagement of sorts, of one year or until the marked reaches the age of consent—eighteen in your case."

"And then what?"

"At the end of that term, if you agreed, he would then

claim you, make you his own—similar to marriage." She pats my hand.

"And if I didn't want to be claimed? What then?"

"You'd be turned over to the proper authorities," says Keegan. "And the wait would've been in vain."

"If I agreed to marking, I'd have until the age of eighteen—two more years—to figure this all out. I mean, we could come up with something else. Right?"

"In theory, yes." Keegan takes in a deep breath then rubs his jaw. "But even if Ethan were to leave his mark, it wouldn't be enough."

"I don't understand." My gaze bounces from Keegan to my grandmother and then back to Keegan. "But you all said—"

"He's not high enough in the clan"—Cole pops his fingers, one at a time—"Or old enough. He'd need approval from his eldest living family member, as well as the blessing of the alpha leader of the clan."

"His mother and Keegan?" A headache throbs behind my left eye.

"No, the eldest living *male* member'a approval. In this case, since our father didn't have any brothers, that'd be me. Not to mention the blessing of Keegan, our alpha."

"You'd also need a high-ranking Wiccan member to sanction the union since you're Kindred." Keegan turns his attention to Agartha.

"Yes. I figured that much." Agartha hovers a few inches off the floor. "Which is why she must be claimed by all three of you."

"Nope. Not gonna happen." I shake my head for emphasis. "I'm not doing that."

I'd like to develop the ability to fly or teleport—then I could get the hell out of here.

I back away from Agartha, inching closer to the middle of the couch. "I'm not about to let everyone in this room bite me. And just so you all know, sex is off the table, completely. I am so not going there or doing that. Not happening. Period."

"It is true, all three must mark you," chuckles Agartha. "But you needn't sexually join with any of them." Her cheeks hold a rosy glow. "They only need to bite you to seal the deal."

My jaw drops. Did I hear her right? *Sure, bite the new girl—the more the merrier.*

"Hey." Cole holds up his arms. "I didn't say I was—"

"Silence." Keegan's voice booms, and the room falls silent. "If turned over, what will happen to the girl? She has the right to know?"

"As an anomaly"—Agartha casts her gaze to the floor

"Anomaly." I choke on the word. "What the fuck! There's nothing abnormal about me."

"Now is the time to listen." Agartha shushes me with the wave of a hand. "The Order seeks to use you for breeding, to see if they can produce additional Kindred offspring by harvesting your eggs, which is no different from what the wolf clans have in mind. Not to mention, the Order has a lab set up. They're ready to study you—to test and measure your abilities as they develop and grow."

Her words leave me grasping for a retort.

"Additional Kindred offspring, male or female, could tip the balance of power in the clans and covens, alike. This could bring an end to all treaties currently in place," says Keegan. "It would rip our culture wide open and expose us to humans."

"Yes, which is why Sadie's grandfather and I protected her all these years." Translucent sparks of light dance on the tips of Agartha's fingers. "If she isn't sheltered by your clan —by being marked or claimed—she'll be taken. And her confinement will stir the workings of a war. So, what will it be? Will you protect her, or incite war and risk the downfall of our culture, or even perpetuate the extinction of our very existence?" She shifts her gaze to Cole. "Even you can't argue that plight."

"Fine. I'll aid in this endeavor." Cole points at me. "But *only* if she agrees."

"What do you say, Ethan?" Agartha extracts a decorative silver tin with leaves etched in it from her purse. "What are your thoughts?" She opens it, grabs a mint like diskette, and then pops it into her mouth.

"I think mine are transparent, but I won't force her either," replies Ethan.

"The question should be answered by the Kindred." Keegan gestures to me. "It doesn't matter what anyone else has to say." He faces me. "It all comes down to what *you* want."

"God. I should've never answered the request to go to the principal's office or listened to the attorney." I draw my knees to my chest and cover my face. "If I hadn't, none of this would've happened."

For a brief moment in Dr. Gus' office, I had considered going on the run, especially after learning about the incarceration of the Greene family. But the lure of meeting family, of finally belonging, had sucked me in.

Now, here I sit with no voice or choice again, which fucking sucks.

"Child." Agartha kneels in front of me. "It was never a question of *if* they would discover you, but a matter of when."

"The witch is right." Keegan glances out the window,

following movement outside.

"Binding your powers offered a bandaid approach. And it was only a matter of time before you encountered both clan and coven members." She clears her throat. "Upon contact with all supernaturals, especially lupines, lycans, and Wiccans, they would have known you were different, and that you're not entirely human."

"What? How?"

"By smell." Ethan scoots back against the couch cushion, placing an arm behind me.

"They'd have known you weren't full lupine either, which would've made you a target." Agartha turns to Ethan. "Help me up, whelp." She extends a hand.

As instructed, Ethan rises and helps my grandmother to her feet.

Grandmother. The word sounds odd, even in the private confines of my head.

"Make a choice child and quickly." Agartha pats my knee. "Time isn't your friend today nor ours."

"Make a *choice,* really?" I shake my head. "There aren't any, not really."

My selections, limited at best, now breathe down my neck like flames slithering around a burning building—consumption's only a matter of time.

One thing's clear. *I don't want to be a lab rat, and I sure as hell don't want to cause a bubbling war, nor to be the blame for countless lives lost, including my own.*

I've already taken one life. Even now, I don't understand why it had to happen in the first place.

Standing on shaky legs, I draw in a deep breath then exhale slowly.

Hmm. A lab rat poked and prodded or marked by a shifter.

"If marked, where would I live?" I can't bring myself to look at the one person in the room who shares a paternal connection with me. "And with whom?"

"Not here." The words tumble out of Cole's mouth.

"The ranch." Agartha places a hand on my shoulder.

I swallow hard, struggling to maintain my composure. "With you?" My words come out barely above a whisper.

"No. Child." She cups my chin and holds my gaze. "With a guardian assigned by the Order."

Pulling away from her touch, I fight the tears threatening to spill over the threshold of my resolve.

"Can't say I'm surprised." I slide away from her as far as I can without running into Ethan. "You didn't want me then, so why should it be any different now?"

"If that is what you think"—she closes the gap between her body and mine—"you understand nothing."

"Really? You tossed me out like a stray."

"All I have done over the years was to keep you safe. Why do you think you ended up here and now? It was to protect you."

"Yeah, right? You didn't even bother to meet me at the house."

She pauses, then lets out a long sigh. "Things didn't turn out as I had hoped, and I cannot change that, but you're here now."

An image of a six by six room with unbreakable glass walls, and a sterile smell, flashes before my eyes. The only structures, a twin bed bolted to the floor and a toilet, offers little to no privacy.

"I'll do it." My voice quivers. "I'll, uhm"—I wipe sweaty palms against my shirt—"I'll submit to being marked, but not claimed. And once it's done"—I hold her gaze—"I want nothing to do with you ever again."

CHAPTER TWELVE

Ethan Cotter

"SO, WHAT HAPPENS NEXT?" Sadie chews on her quivering lower lip.

"Now, I bestow my blessings for this union." Agartha claps her hands together. "There is much to do."

She's agreed to marking, to becoming a member of the clan, which seems like the lesser of the two evils, but I can't help but wonder what complications will grow from that choice.

"I'll let the clans, covens, the Order, and the Creed of Council know the Kindred has until dawn to complete the requirements of the marking ceremony." Agartha makes her way to the door and opens it. "Keegan, you have my blessing. I now leave you and your clan to proceed."

Keegan walks to the door, locks it, and then draws the curtains closed. He approaches Sadie and offers a hand. "You'll need to wear something else."

"Why?" Hesitantly, she takes his hand and stands.

"Because Cole and I will need access to your body to mark you."

She looks from Keegan to me, then back to Keegan. "Wait. Where exactly will you mark me?" Suspicion grows on her face along with a hint of apprehension.

"Here." Keegan presses a finger to his chest. "About three inches down from your collarbone."

"Give me a minute. I have an idea." Cole walks out of the room. When he returns, he's carrying a plush, white bath towel. "You can wrap this around your upper body."

Sadie takes the towel from Cole.

"Uhm. I'll be back." She retrieves the sports bra from the coffee table and tucks it between the towel.

"Where're you going?" Keegan brushes a curtain to the side and peers out the window.

"Bathroom." Turning away, she makes her way down the hall. The click of the door lock resonates.

"This is all kinds of fucked up." Cole paces, walking a straight line from the hall to the kitchen and back.

"Calm your inner wolf," says Keegan over his shoulder. "It could be worse."

"Yeah. How's that?" Cole pauses his trek for a few seconds, waiting for me to move out of the way.

"Your mother could be home." A slight grin tugs at Keegan's lips.

Cole glances at the watch on his wrist. "Her shift was over hours ago."

"Yeah. She's lock up tight in the diner doing inventory"—Keegan rubs his jaw—"unaware of what happening under her roof."

"Man." His mother losing her shit isn't something he's looking forward to. "She's gonna go off like a nuclear explosion when she finds out."

"And it's your fault, again." Cole jabs a finger into my chest."

"What the hell would you have me do? Turn her over? Fuck that? They'd do all kinds of shit to her. Experiments."

"Enough. No one's touching her." Keegan's voice booms. "So, stop the fuckin' bickering."

What the hell have I gotten her into?

The bathroom door clicks, and the living room falls silent.

Her steps, slow and irregular, draw closer. At the entrance from the hall, she stops. She's wearing the towel tucked around her body, and the shirt hangs from her hand. The straps of her pink sports bra stand out against her skin.

"Come here." Keegan motions for her to approach.

Sadie makes her way over to where Keegan and Cole now stand. I'm not sure if I should join them or wait.

"Uhm." A tremor makes her hands shake. "Will I become like those things . . . the ones at Roman's?" Fear keeps her in place.

"No, because you are Kindred." I guide her to the edge of the chaise.

Fear wafts around her, melding with her sweet aroma. Back on the road, I had noticed the unfamiliar scent but couldn't place it. And now I know why.

"Lie down with your head at the foot of the chaise." Keegan's voice has a soft timber to it, a tone I'm unaccustomed to. "You can close your eyes if you prefer."

She shakes her head. "No. I want to see."

"Very well." Keegan places a hand on her shoulder and one on her hip. "Then with this mark, I welcome you into the Shoshone clan." His cobalt blue eyes turn a coppery, golden color. Ushering a low, throaty growl, he exposes his teeth, and his canines grow in length.

"What the fuck?" Sadie squirms on the furniture.

"Ethan. Hold her." Keegan's voice has a raspy tone to it that it didn't have before.

"Wait. Please." Sadie's eyes brim with tears. She struggles to sit up.

"Have you changed your mind?" Cole speaks up. "Would you rather take your chances with those outside?"

"Uhm. No. I'm just . . . I need a—"

Ethan kneels on the other side of the chaise. "Look at me. It sounds worse than it is. He'll make it quick, they both will, I promise." I stroke her face.

"Okay." Sadie raises her arms and places them above her head.

With unspoken words, I nod to my brethren to continue.

"Calm yourself." Cole kneels at the base of the chaise and cups her wrists in the palm of his hands.

"Yeah." Sadie's eyes widen. "That's easy for you to say. You're doing the biting."

"Don't take your eyes off me," I say, softly. "Just keep them on me."

Lowering his head, Keegan sinks his right canine into the soft folds of her flesh.

"Holy shit." Sadie cries out but doesn't break eye contact with me. "Fuckity, fuck."

The wolf within feels conflicted. On one hand, it's pleased she's going through the marking ceremony, but on the other, anger stirs deep because the process creates pain.

Her fear, now palpable in spades, pulls at me.

"You're next." Keegan rises but keeps his hold on Sadie.

Cole kneels next to her. "With this mark, I too, welcome you into the Shoshone clan, sister." He lowers his head and pierces her flesh.

When Cole stands, Keegan releases Sadie's arms.

Peering down, Sadie spies two circular marks to the side of her covered breast next to the pink bra strap. Blood pools in the shallow dips.

"I'm bleeding." She gingerly touches the two pin dot wounds.

"Not for long." Leaning over her, I gently lick the wounds.

"What are you doing?" Sadie winces and shoves me. "They'll get infected."

"Don't push me away." I cradle her face. "My saliva will help the skin heal."

A boom, followed by a thunderous clash outside, rattles the windows.

"What the hell was that?" Sadie jumps, bumping her head into mine.

"Put it on." Cole picks the Tee-shirt up off the floor and tosses it at Sadie, who pulls it over her head.

"Careful. Don't touch them, or they'll scar." I turn my focus to Keegan. "What the fuck's going on out there?"

"Don't know." Keegan peers out the window. "But we're about to find out."

"What do you see?" Sadie glances over a shoulder, straining to peek out the window.

"Nothing for either of you to worry about." Keegan motions for Cole to approach. "It's time we took our leave." He makes his way to the door, then locks eyes with me. "You have until the break of dawn to fulfill the requirements of either the marking ceremony or to claim her as a mate. That's all I can give you."

"Understood." I watch until both men walk out of the door.

"What now?" Fear wafts around her.

CHAPTER THIRTEEN

Sadie Reed

BURSTS OF BLUE LIGHT hit the window.

Glass shards fly across the room.

"Get down." Ethan slides off the furniture, pulling me with him.

Searing heat burns my cheek. I skim a hand across my face and view crimson fluid covering my fingertips. "I'm bleeding."

Slivers of glass sparkle on the floor, reflecting the beams of lights shooting across the room.

"What the hell?" I kneel and peer out the window. "Where are they coming from?"

A line of cape-wearing men and woman form a line in the front yard. Glowing orbs of energy spin a few inches above their palms.

"Who are they?"

A luminescent ball of energy shoots through the window and across the room, heading in my direction.

"That'd be some of the Order." Ethan tackles me to the ground. "The Rodeseus coven. They're fuckin' fanatics."

The door blows open, smacks the wall, and then swings, hanging off a single hinge.

"Surrender the Kindred," a man looms inside the door. "Or I will come and get it."

"It?" The word floats around in my head. "What the fuck is wrong with you people?"

"Stay down," Ethan whispers in my ear.

You call a piece of furniture it—or a spider, or insect, I think to myself, *not a person.*

"I have a name, asshole." I wiggle under the weight of Ethan's frame, trying to break free. "Get off me."

"Give *it* to me, and we will leave."

"Can't do that." Keegan peers through the shattered window. "The Kindred is under the protection of the Shoshone clan." He leaps over the sill, landing inside the house. "My protection."

"You're not welcome on Cotter land, Samuel Wardwell." Cole springs through the window, landing next to Keegan. "Little Brother. Sadie. Go, now."

"Cole and I have each left our mark on the girl." Keegan keeps his eyes trained on Samuel. "Under the treaty, she has until dawn to accept a final mark from the whelp, Ethan."

"*It* has no rights." Samuel holds his hand out in front of him, palm up. "The Rodeseus cove have come to collect." A glowing orb materializes. He manipulates it with his fingers, and it grows.

Wind blows through the house, sending Samuel and the orb tumbling across the floor.

A funnel of luminescent smoke swirls, reminding me of a dust devil, but only this one's indoors and glowing.

"What's that?" I raise a hand to shield my eyes from the bright lights the tornadic spiral gives off.

"Samuel Wardwall of the Rodeseus coven, you are not welcome here." Agartha hovers a foot off the ground. Her eyes lack color, they're void of irises and a stark white coloration.

"Release me." Samuel floats weightless above the living room floor.

"How's she doing that?" I smooth some flyaway locks, pulling them into a bun, and then secure my hair with a ponytail holder.

"Magic." Ethan stands, dragging me to my feet. "We gotta go."

"Where?"

"Out back." In an open stride, Ethan takes off running.

I sprint, keeping a close distance behind him.

"Go." He turns at the end of a hallway and pushes me in front of him. "Cole's bedroom."

"Where?" I'm shoved into a room.

"Don't stop." He glances over his shoulder at the door leading to the hallway. "Head for the south wall."

"What?" Glancing round, I see a dresser, bed, television, and a covered sliding glass door. I make a dash for it, draw the blinds, and then stumble back into Ethan.

"There's a—" My heart hammers in my chest.

A man looms on the other side of the glass. He slides the door open and takes hold of my wrist.

CHAPTER FOURTEEN

Ethan Cotter

"ETHAN." Panic etches the single word, and she struggles to free herself from Toby Tekin's grip—the alpha of the Lakota clan.

The pungent scent of fear mixes with her alluring essence. The aroma grows by the second and now travels on the currents of the wind, which will draw unwanted attention, I'm sure of it.

"Easy, now." Toby drags Sadie outside. "Not gonna hurt you."

A familiar smell fills my nose, sending my inner beast to the edge of frenzy.

The bones in my hands and feet creak, pop, and then begin to shift. Pre-transformation warms my body from the inside out. Blood rushes to my head, pounding in my ears.

"Control yourself." Toby grabs my shirt and lifts me off the ground. "Focus. You can't help her if you don't contain your beast."

I reel in my wolf and concentrate my energies on keeping a human form.

Shadows beyond the yard snake in and out of view. Red glowing eyes appear in the darkness, announcing the arrival of a lycan pack—a rogue one at that.

"Beyond the trees . . ." I call on the eyes of my beast.

My vision brightens, and an amber tint sharpens the view of the dense, wooded area.

Five bipedal lycans, clan less and rogue by scent, stalk forward in formation. One slinks down the center with two of his pack hanging back three yards behind him. Those on the outside of the formation steal away into the darkness.

"They're trying to flank us." I keep my focus on the center beast who continues to gain ground.

"Yeah. Noticed." A hint of amusement coats Toby's calm tone. "They won't get far."

"You know him?" Sadie's shoulders roll forward, and she ceases her struggle for release.

"Yes." I place a hand on the small of her back. "He's with us."

"Is he a . . . uhm creature like—"

"Lupine. He's an alpha like Keegan."

"Toby Tekin. Call me Toby."

"How many leaders are there?"

"One per clan." Toby holds her gaze. "I'm Alpha of the Lakota." He sniffs the surrounding air, and his eyes glow a coppery hue. "Well, now, you smell different, don't ya?"

"Uhm. Perfume?" Sadie inhales a ragged breath.

"No. That's all you." Toby takes in another whiff, and the hue of his eyes burn brighter.

A ping of jealousy makes my shoulders tense. *Mine*, the wolf within me whispers.

"Sam and Troy with you?" I struggle to keep my inner beast in check.

"They're in the woods, hunting rogues."

The clomp of horse hooves echoes in my ears. Even with my boots on, the tremors of the animals' steps vibrate underfoot.

"Ever ride a horse?" Toby whistles a bird call through parsed lips.

"Uhm. A-a few times." She swallows hard.

"Good." He glances over a shoulder. "Charlie here will get you setup. Won't you?"

Charles Ince, known in small circles as *Charlie-the-mute-horse-empath*, came to Kensington Cove as a lone stray. Up in age and being the last of an extinct clan from New Mexico, made it hard for him to join the ranks of most packs. But Toby took him in with open arms.

Leading three horses by the reins, Charlie tips a cowboy hat, and then offers a warm smile. With a wave of a hand, he motions for her to approach.

"Wait." Sadie's eyes widen, making the whites stand out like two little round moons against a starless sky. "I'm getting on that—alone?"

Another layer of fear wafts in the air around her.

"No. You'll ride with someone." Toby relinquishes his hold on her wrist.

He hands her over to me as if passing her off to my care once again.

"Mount up. We haven't much time. My clan and Keegan's can hold off the rogues, but the Wiccans are a whole other story."

I mount one of the three horses, then take the leather leads from Charlie. "Come on." I offer an outstretched arm to Sadie.

"I-I can't ride that." She stumbles into Toby, who keeps her on her feet.

A snarl, followed by a forlorn cry, pierces the night.

Sadie jumps and glances over her shoulder at the open sliding glass door leading to Cole's room.

"Let's go. You don't have time to ponder what if scenarios." Toby half-leads, half drags her to the horse. "Take his hand." He slips my boot out of the stirrup and smacks the top with his palm. "Step here, and he'll pull you up."

Going through the motions outlined by Toby, Sadie places a bare foot on top of my rattlesnake boot.

One quick tug, and she slips on to the saddle in front of me.

"Hold on." I draw her upright in the seat.

Relief settles over me with her this close, but it's short lived because rogues stalk her from the shadows.

"To what?" She trembles on the seat. "There's nothing to grab."

"The mane, the saddle horn, or me. Anything is fair game but the leads."

Toby mounts, followed by Charlie.

"Head out." Toby whistles, and the horses snort, then take off in a trot—mine in the middle and Charlie's brings up the rear.

"Wait. We can't see." She squirms on the seat.

"Maybe you can't"—Toby clicks his tongue twice and his horse picks up speed—"But we can." His eyes glow a coppery hue which match Charlie's.

Less than five minutes out, rogue lycans in more of a mutated wolf's form than human's flank the line, snapping at the horses with elongated, malformed muzzles.

The horses pick up speed, but the rogues isolate my steed from the rest of the group.

Howls break out from the west and northeast.

"A-are those lycans?" I can't tell if she's trembling or the full trot is tossing her about. "Or lupines—friendlies?"

"Back up. More of Keegan's clan."

Sadie bounces on the seat. She releases the mane, seizes the saddle horn, but then loses her grasp.

"I'm going to fall." She grabs my thighs with both hands. Holding on with a firm grip she digs her nails into the denim fabric.

"I got you." I wrap an arm around her, drawing her against my body and back in the seat.

A wall of lupines in wolf form converge.

"Oh, God, there's more of them." The wind mutes Sadie's words.

Leaping into the air, the lupines transform into bipedal weremen, taking the rogues down.

Charlie flanks my horse on the right. Shotgun in hand, he fires off a round, taking down a lycan in mid-leap.

"Don't squeeze the horse with your legs," I whisper in her ear. "Relax and let them set against mine or hook your feet around my calves."

"Uhm. Okay."

Toby trots up. "You two okay?"

"Yeah." Doing a quick spot check, I glance over one shoulder, then the other. Open pasture fills my vision.

Thirty minutes into the ride, she slumps against me, allowing her body to move with the motion of the horse instead of working against it.

"Better?" Inhaling her scent, I pick up trace particles of cortisol, indicating her stress level remains high.

"Yeah, kind of." Her hands, still on my thighs, no long hold on with a death grip. "Where are we going?"

"If guessing, to a cave in the mouth of the mountain on the north side of Keegan's property."

"Why there?" Her breaths now match mine.

"Because the rogues won't follow." My arm cradles her, keeping her pressed against me. Hand held against her midriff, I relish the warmth of her flesh under my fingertips.

"Why not?" The smooth skin of the side of her face brushes against my lips.

"It's sacred."

"Oh." She releases her grip on my right thigh, lays her arm on mine, and then laces her fingers with mine.

At the base of a ravine, a mountain comes into view.

"See that?" I point at a trail cut into the side of the formation.

"Yeah, but it's hard to see." She leans forward on the seat.

Cool air rushes between my body and hers, punctuating the loss of heat.

"Is that where we're going?"

"Yes. From here, we climb."

Drawing the leads back, I bring the horse to a full stop, and then dismount.

"Come here." I hold out my arms. "Swing your leg over."

Sadie sits sidesaddle and then slides into my open arms. When her feet hit the ground, I draw her close, holding her in a firm embrace.

"What if they're waiting? Hiding in the dark?"

"I'd know."

I draw in a deep breath, filling my lungs. Traces of geckos, wild pigs, skunks, coyotes, and other small game register.

"How?" She clings to me.

"By smell."

"Hey. I'll come for you when it's safe to return to your place." The words echo, bouncing off the stone surface of the mountain. "We're going to clear the area. Sentries are nearby if needed."

"Thanks, Toby. I owe you—both of you."

"That you do, whelp." Toby ushers a series of whistles and all three horses trot off, leaving me alone with Sadie in the dark.

CHAPTER FIFTEEN

Sadie Reed

A BLACK VOID of nothingness surrounds me.

Even with the breeze blowing, air hunger forces me to inhale, but each breath lacks satisfaction.

"Come on." He tugs my hand, urging me forward. "The cave isn't far."

Focusing, I shadow his steps, hoping to avoid tripping hazards, sharp rocks, thorns, and creepy crawlers of the night.

I stumble over something hard, then slide off the side of a rock into something prickly. An explosion of burning pain ignites across the sole of my foot.

"Ooh. Fuck." I hobble on one foot, stubbing my toe. "Double fuck."

Ethan releases my hand and looks back. "You okay?"

"Yeah. Sort of." I slip and fall into him.

"Careful." He steps in front of me, giving me his back. "Jump on."

"What?"

"You heard me." He squats. "Get on."

The thought of pressing my body so intimately against his, makes my cool flesh flush, sending a wave of warmth rushing from head to toe.

"It beats walking." Ethan takes a knee, then offers a hand.

I wrap an arm around his neck, and using my legs, I brace my body on his back. His warmth offers a welcome change from the cool night air.

"Uhm. You sure you can get up there with me like this."

"Yeah." He rises, takes a few steps, and then does a slow shuffle. "And it'll be faster."

I hug him close, pressing my chest against him. Thoughts of the kiss—his touch—enter my mind.

In the span of forty-eight hours, a lot of shit has gone down. The Greene family's incarceration, leaving friends and my high school behind, moving to a small town, inheriting a house of horrors, discovering lupines, lycans, and witches exist, and even with all that newfound information, I feel a connection—a sense of belonging in Kensington Cove.

I'm Shoshone now, or almost, whatever that means.

The two shallow puncture marks—bites from Cole and Keegan—tingle.

Marked? What about claimed by a wolf, a lupine? Would it be so bad? Hmm. Claiming would require . . .

The thought of skin on skin in the thralls of, well sex, makes my body flush again. That's a huge leap from no base to fully on the board, traveling around all the mounds of the diamond at once, so to speak.

Ethan draws in a slow, deep breath.

"What's on your mind?" His words have an underline growl to them.

"Stuff. Lots and lots of stuff."

"Like what?" Another growl starts deep in his chest. "Tell me."

"San Antonio. Moving. My car. What happened at Roman's house. Knowing supernatural beings exist . . ."

"And?" His body, which was warm moments ago, feels hot as if he's core temperature has increased.

"That's all. Nothing else."

"You know I'm a lupine, right?"

"Uhm, yes. What's your point?"

"I have an enhanced sense of smell." He sniffs the air.

I glance first to the right, then left. Darkness fills my vision. "Is it them? Are they back?" Panic causes the flutters in my belly to take flight. "Do you smell them?"

"No." A chuckle passes his lip. "I smell your lust." He enters the mouth of the cave.

"Well, I think your senses went haywire."

Inside the cave, I slide off. At once, I feel a void, a loss of heat from his body.

His footsteps track deeper into the dark chamber.

"Uhm. Ethan." My heartbeat picks up speed. "I don't want to be—"

A clang rattles, echoing around me.

I take a step forward, turn and then head to the opening of the cave. The primal need for light drives me forward in search of the moon.

"Where do you think you're going?"

CHAPTER SIXTEEN

Ethan Cotter

LIGHT FLASHES at her feet.

She whips around, shields her eyes, and slams into me.

"How?" Confusion etches her face. "Where'd you get that?"

"This?" I hold up a lit lantern.

"Yeah."

"From the prepping kit about a hundred yards in." I take her hand in mine, coaxing her inside the cave. "Thirsty? There's water."

A howl pierces the night, followed by another one a few seconds later.

She nods but doesn't speak a single word.

My inner wolf stands on alert, ready to act.

"What if the rogue lycans don't care this is sacred ground?" Taking the lantern in hand, she scans the area. "With only one way in"—she peeks around a narrow corner

—"if they rush inside, we'll be trapped." Crossing the chamber, she checks another tunnel. "Captured."

"Hey." I intercept her at the mouth of another opening.

"That's a dead end, too."

"We're safe in here." I draw her into my arms. "Toby assigned sentries."

"What if they leave? Or those things get them?" A light sheen covers her forehead. "We need another way out."

"Hey. Look at me." Fear wafts around her, pungent and thick. "We're not trapped, and Sadie, I won't let anything happen to you."

Her breaths, fast and shallow, keep beat with the racing cadence of her heart thumping in her chest.

She's gonna hyperventilate if she keeps this up, I think to himself.

"Slow your breathing." Inhaling a controlled and steady breath, I model some deep breathing, and she follows the example. "That's good. In . . . One, two, three." I pause for a couple of seconds. "Out . . . Four, five, six."

The rise and fall of her chest slows.

"You okay?"

"Yeah," she replies barely above a whisper. "Sorry. Didn't mean to flake out."

"It's all good." I take the lantern from her hand. "Come here. I want to show you something."

Lacing my fingers with hers, I guide her to the west side of the cave, containing the prepping kit.

Flipping the locks open on a trunk, I pull out a blanket and then spread it out.

"Water?" I offer her a bottle.

"Thanks." She takes it from my hand.

"Come here." I sit, then pat a spot next to me. "I don't bite."

Her brows shoot up, and a small smile rolls across her lips.

"Wow. I can't believe you just said that?"

Slowly, she brushes off the bottom of her bare feet and then plops on the blanket.

She draws her knees to her chest. "So, you're really going there?"

Fear still lingers, swirling around her, just not as heavy as before. His inner beast, highly attuned to the clues her body gives off, stands on high alert. The wolf lies in wait, ready to spring into action at a moment's notice if a need for action presents itself.

A wolfish grin rolls across my lips. "In my defense, you started the line of thought."

"And how do you figure that?" She holds my gaze.

"Your lustful thoughts when on my back."

A crimson blush covers her face, neck, and ears. "I wasn't—"

I tip her chin and draw her in so close; I can almost feel her lips on mine.

She holds my gaze. Her tongue slides over her lips, and she closes the small gap.

"What were you thinking?" My mouth brushes against hers. "Tell me."

"Uhm." Her lids flutter, sending her lashes fanning across her high cheekbones.

"Was it this?" I press my mouth against hers, then nibble on her lower lip. "Or this?" I coax her to open to me, and when her lips part, I plunge my tongue inside, deepening the intensity of the kiss.

Sliding a hand down her arm, I draw her to my chest and ease her on to the blanket.

"I want to touch you." My arm rests on her hip. "Taste

you." I trace the hem of the boxers with the tips of my fingers.

She chews on the inside of her lower lip, enticing the wolf.

Stretching out beside her, I hold her doe-eyed gaze.

"O-okay." The word comes out with a squeak.

A wolfish grin washes across my face. The beast howls a silent call, excitement building.

Rolling her hip back, I guide her into a prone position, and then skim a hand across her stomach.

Her abdominal muscles contract under my touch.

A nervous giggle escapes her lips, and her eyes brighten.

I trace the edge of the boxers from her belly button to the hollow of a hip.

A nervous energy swirls around her, and a wave of goosebumps erupt from her toes to the top of her head.

"Your bead . . ." She touches the stubble on my face. "It tickles."

Pressing my mouth to her neck, I leave a trail of kisses to her mouth.

"Uhm." She trembles in my arms, and then a soft moan escapes her lips.

"You like that?"

She nods, and then wraps her arms around my neck, drawing me closer.

Claiming her lips once again, I slip a hand to the band of the boxers and toy with the edge of the fabric. Slowly, I dip the tip of a finger under the elastic.

Her heart pounds in her chest as if seeking an exit.

"Wait. Uhm." In a flash, her hand shoots down, halting my exploration.

"Am I moving too fast?" Breathing in her scent, a mixture of lust and anxiety wafts around her.

She nods her head but avoids eye contact, so I tip her chin until her eyes meet mine.

"Breathe." Moving my hand from her hip to her face, I caress her cheek. "We can go as slow as you want." I kiss her cheek. "You call the shots. Okay?"

"Can we just lay here? Like this?" She places her head on my chest.

"Yeah." The wolf in me listens to the thumping of her heart as it slows to a steady beat.

Slowly, he whispers in my thoughts. *Don't scare away.*

I cradle her in my arms.

A single thought replays in my mind, will she agree to the bite?

I yearn to mark her—claim her.

My inner wolf sniffs her neck. *Mine*, the word resonates in the recesses of my mind.

Closing my eyes, I'm left wondering . . . *Is it the wolf who claims a mate by marking, or does the mate claim the wolf in heart, body, and soul?*

CHAPTER SEVENTEEN

Sadie Reed

A STEADY BREATH BLOWS warmth across my neck.

My eyes snap open, and I lock gazes with Ethan.

"I, uhm"—I cover a yawn with the back of a hand—"must've dosed off."

"A little." Ethan repositions his body and rolls to his side.

He draws me close and presses his lips to mine. The kiss deepens, and he caresses the side of my face. His body tenses, and a low, throaty growl rumbles in his chest.

He springs to his feet, leaving me alone on the blanket.

"What is it?" I sit, hugging my knees to my chest.

Fear rekindles in my belly, twisting my insides into tight knots.

"Shh." He motions for me to remain silent.

A shadow snakes along the walls of the cave.

The piercing sound of a whistle echoes inside the cavern.

"Whelp." Toby's voice booms around me. "Time to go."

Ethan offers a hand. "Come on."

"Go where?" I set my hand in his.

"About to find out." He draws me to my feet and into his arms. "Toss the blanket in the trunk."

Grabbing the corners, I half-fold it, and then return it to where it came from.

"What is all this?" Inside the trunk, first aid supplies, MREs, clothing, and some crude cookware take up space next to the blanket—each in airtight packages.

"Prep kit. Remember?" He turns the dial on the lantern, and the glow of the flame decreases to a thin, ruddy hue.

"Prep? Yeah, looks more like 'on-the-run' shit stashed in a cave."

"That too." A chuckle passes his lips.

"Any time now." Annoyance etches Toby's voice.

"Comin'." Ethan heads to the mouth of the cave, and I follow on his heels.

The flat stone underfoot contains a smooth texture. Thoughts of the rocks, prickly plants, and dirt outside make me shudder.

Damn. What I'd do for a pair of shoes right now. I take in my mode of dress. *And some fucking clothes, too.*

"Charlie." Looming just outside of the entrance, stands Toby. "We head out in five," he shouts over a shoulder.

Twenty yards away, Charlie mans the same horses from prior.

Toby draws in a deep breath, filling his lungs. He looks from Ethan to me, and then back to Ethan.

"It'll be dawn in"—Toby glances at the watch on his wrist—"two hours." He pauses. "You wear his scent, but no mark." His eyes land on Ethan. "Care to explain?"

"We were getting' around to it." Ethan runs a hand

through his hair. "Just haven't gotten to that point yet. And I have until sunrise."

"Cutting it close, don't you think?" Toby heads down the side of the mountain. Five feet out, darkness swallows him.

A chill slinks up the length of my spine. The sensation of eyes watching me from a distance makes me shiver.

"What if those things are out there?"

Ethan leaps to a rock below. "The rogues?" He offers a hand.

"Yeah." I sit on the edge of a bolder and slides into his arms.

"Get on." Ethan kneels, offering his back.

Without hesitation, I take him up on the offer.

It beats stepping on prickly things that sting.

"Don't waste energy worrying about the lycans," Toby calls out from the darkness.

"Why not?" The warmth of Ethan's body offers a layer of comfort I find calming.

"Because they're not who *you* need to concern yourself with."

"Oh, yeah?" I search the night, but only darkness blooms six feet out. "Who then?"

"That'd be the Wiccans."

CHAPTER EIGHTEEN

Ethan Cotter

MINE, my inner wolf whispers. *Protect mate.*

I focus on keeping my beast at bay.

She's not ours yet—transformation with Sadie on my back isn't the way I want to introduce her to him—*but soon, real soon, she'll be mine—theirs.*

The gums around my canines tingle, itching to elongate. And the warmth of her body pressing intimately against mine, makes my dick strain against the jeans.

Fuck. Get a grip.

"Hold on." I tug on her arm, and she tightens her embrace.

I clear the last thirty feet of the descent with ease, leaping from rock to rock. At the base, I land next to Toby, and then do a shuffle to the waiting horses.

Sadie slides off my back then fidgets with the shirt hem, avoiding Toby's gaze.

Her uneasiness sets my beast off. "If you have something to say"—I direct my words at Toby—"spit it out."

"What did you decide?" Toby stares her down.

"That's not any of your—"

Even in the darkness, the flush on her face shines.

"I disagree." Toby checks the belt of the saddle I rode on with Sadie earlier. "Me and my pack answered a call to arms." He looks up, locking on to her gaze. "Lost a good man in the scrimmage."

Holding out the reins, he relinquishes them to me.

"The way I see it, I have every right to know your decision—as does everyone else."

Silence blankets the night.

"So, what's it gonna be?" Toby mounts his horse. "You a lab rat?"

"Fuck off." She spits the words out with defiance and a touch of venom.

The corners of Toby's lips quirk. "Shoshone it is."

My inner wolf grins. Her spunk and tenacity in the face of the unknown intrigues both me and my wolf.

Back at Roman's house during the attack, she had embraced fear head on instead of allowing it to break her. Yet, back in the cave, she had a moment of weakness. But even then, she overcame it.

Now, I understand why. She carries Roman's lineage— an ancient lupine line.

Swinging a leg over, I mount the horse, reach over, and then pull Sadie on to the saddle in front of me.

Anger along with something else swirls around her—a scent I'm not sure how to classify. It's the same aroma I had noticed during the attack.

Her aroma, not lupine in nature but most definitely supernatural in origin, coats her body like a second skin.

Wiccan, my wolf whispers. *Old and ancient, it is.*

The ravine leads into an open pasture of flat land, it's the same area the lycan's only hours ago had launched a sneak attack.

Memories of the rogues snapping at Sadie's bare feet and exposed legs, feeds the anger brewing in my gut, which in turn, nourishes my beast's hatred for any all who seek to harm what is mine.

I trot up next to Toby. "What of Samuel? The Order?"

"Agartha took him and his coven down a few notches. Ain't that so, Charlie?"

A smile of satisfaction rolls across Charlie's face, and he nods.

"They're camped out on the front lawn and as docile as newborn kittens."

"What?" Sadie places a hand on my thigh and leans in Toby's direction. "How?"

"Binding spell." Toby whistles and the horses pick up speed. "Let's ride." He casts a glance at Sadie. "Destine awaits."

CHAPTER NINETEEN

Sadie Reed

"ARROGANT ASS," she whispers the words under her breath.

"I've been called many things, Sadie Reed." Laughter erupts on Toby's lips. "That doesn't even rank in the top five."

"Do you try to piss people off"—the desire to wipe the smile from his face grows—"or is it a God-given gift?"

"I like this one, whelp." Toby pulls ahead, taking the lead. "Hope you haven't bitten off more than you can handle," he says over his shoulder.

"Oh, my God. Is he always like this?" I wiggle on the saddle seat, repositioning the hem of the boxers. "And why's he calling you a whelp? Isn't that a puppy?"

"It's like calling someone younger a kid or runt, it's an endearment. You'll hear it a lot in the lupine and lycan communities." He leans next to my head and draws in a breath, filling his lungs.

"Did you just smell my hair?"

"No. Your scent. It has a spicy tang to it when you're angry."

I turn just enough to lock gazes with him. His irises, once a smoky blue, contain the coppery, glowing hue from earlier.

Wonder if that's how he can see in the darkness?

If he and the wolf are one and the same, does that mean he can view things through the eyes of his—*what did he call it*—his beast.

He wraps an arm around my waist, drawing me against him. "He likes you."

"Who?"

"Toby." The increasing warmth of his body makes me conscious of how close we both now sit.

"Why do you say that?"

"Because usually, you can't get two words out of the guy."

A light flickers, blinking in the dark night.

One of Toby's comments surfaces in my brain: *hope you haven't bitten off more than you can handle.*

Bitten—the word brings on a wave of anxiety that makes my palms sweat and sends butterflies flying without direction in the pit of my belly.

"You okay?" The soft stubble of his emerging beard tickles the side of my face.

"Yeah. I'm fine."

"You sure about that? Apprehension wafts all around you and has you jumpier than a rabbit in a den of wolves."

"Nice choice of words there, Romeo." Toby slows, allowing the horses to travel side by side. "We'll enter from the north, then travel around to the front door."

"But you said the, uhm"—she searches her brain for the

right words—"Order, covens, clans—hell, whatever the witches call themselves, occupy the front yard."

"They do." Toby whistles a different bird call, and the horses go from a trot to a brisk walk. "Without magic, they're as good as castrated."

"For how long?" Ethan relaxes his hold.

"Until dawn . . ."—Toby's focus falls on me—"pending your decision, Ms. Reed."

Toby trots off. "Get the gate, Charlie."

Choices. I've never really had them before. In the foster care system, others dictate where you live, what you eat and wear, and what you can or can't do. Life had been hard in many ways, but making decisions never kicked off angst because that was something outside of my control.

But this is different. The choice is mine. Fuck. Fuckity fuck!

Becoming a prized science experiment doesn't rank high on my list of things to do.

Or a fucking breeding sack for the witches or other groups. The thought crowds my mind.

Marked. Would it be so bad? Ethan's been by my side. His loyalty never wavering, not even once.

I could do worse, right?

"Okay."

"Okay, what?"

"I'll do it." I swallow hard, keeping the sliver of courage left from escaping on my breath. "I'll submit to marking. You can do it."

Silences falls between me and Ethan. His steady breaths now the only sound echoing in my ears.

The horse follows a trail through an opened gate, snakes around the acre lot making up the yard, and then comes to a full stop next to the front door.

Groups of people linger, keeping their eyes on Agartha. Many of them whisper, but their speech remains just out of reach. I'm left wondering if any of the women gawking are Cole and Ethan's mother.

Agartha approaches. "You returned unmarked, or so I hear." Keegan and Cole stand on each side of her. "Has a decision been reached?"

"Yes. She'll—"

"No." Agartha holds up a hand. "The words must come from the Kindred, Sadie Reed. So, tell me, child, what *sayeth* you?"

Those in attendance stand motionless, their conversations fall silent.

Ethan dismounts and helps me down.

"I submit to marking." I step on the sidewalk.

"By whom?" Agartha flips one side of the cape over her shoulder. "What clan?"

"Shoshone. By Ethan." I pause, wondering why she asked the question, and then recall the on-lookers—*must be a formal thing*. "Ethan Cotter."

"And do you accept her submission, whelp?" A slight curl tugs at the corners of Agartha's mouth.

"I do."

Agartha takes hold of Ethan's hand in one of hers, and mine in the other, and raises them above her head.

"Let it be known to all, the Kindred, Sadie Reed, now joins the Shoshone clan. Under the laws of the marking ceremony, approved and sanctioned by me, Keegan—the alpha of the Shoshone Clan—and Cole Cotter, Sadie now falls under the protection of her brethren and the Order."

"An assault on her"—Keegan steps forward—"is a direct attack on me and my clan."

My temples throb. I'm done playing fish in a bowl. Movement to my left catches my eye.

Samuel Wardwall zeros, holding me in his seething gaze.

"May I go in the house?" My lower lip trembles.

"But of course." Agartha nods, then gestures toward the door.

Inside, shielded from those on the yard, I'm able to release the tension in my shoulders.

I plop on the couch, wishing this was all a bad dream. But the ticking of the clock on the wall says otherwise. It offers a countdown to the approaching dawn.

"You okay?" Ethan slides on the couch next to me.

"What do *you* think?" My words come out harsher than I had anticipated. "I'm sorry. I didn't mean to—"

"It's fine." He tucks a loose strand of hair behind my ear. "There's a lot to take in."

His touch offers the promise of comfort. Something I'm not used to relying on others for, so it feels odd, foreign even.

Thoughts of the cave come to mind, and my face flushes.

In truth, I wish I were still there, away from everyone and everything. In the confines of the cavern, it was only the two of us—the weight of the outside world held at bay.

"Hey." He caresses the side of my face. "I need only mark you, nothing else. You don't have to do anything you're not ready or willing to do. Okay?"

I nod in response, riding a rollercoaster of emotions that flip as easily as a coin flicked into the air.

Heads: dive headfirst into a relationship I'm in over my head with, or Tails: turn tail and run as far as my legs can take me, licking my wounds in the process, or at least until caught and tossed inside a six by six sterile cell.

His smoky, blueish eyes draw me in. There's no malice, anger, or hidden motives to see. Instead, what I view conveys a gentle calmness, an inner peace I long to hold on to.

"W-what if"—I push hair out of his eyes—"What if I want more?" I lean in, brushing my lips against his.

CHAPTER TWENTY

Ethan Cotter

CLAIMING HER MOUTH, I playfully nibble on first her lower lip then upper. When she yields, I deepen the kiss.

Drawing a deep breath, the wolf inside me takes in the scent of her awakening arousal along with a hint of uncertainty.

She seeks freedom and a place to belong, I think to myself. *How do I help her achieve both?*

A need, a deep-seated hunger to protect her, drives me forward.

"C-can we do it somewhere else? The marking?" She peers out the broken window. "Where there's some privacy?"

An audience lines the front lawn.

I don't need the heightened vision of the wolf to know eyes from outside follow every movement between me and Sadie.

"Yeah. We can go to my room." Rising, I draw her into

an embrace, cradling her to my chest. "If that's okay with you."

"Yeah." Her heart beats erratically, and her breaths, short and shallow, release in small bursts. "I'd like that. Anything to get away from them."

I take her by the hand and head across the living room. Shredded fabric from the curtains litter the floor. Shards of glass wink reflected light like twinkling stars.

"Hold up." I scoop her into my arms.

"What are you doing?" She tenses from head to toe.

"Don't want you to cut yourself."

She scans the floor then relaxes against me, placing her head against my shoulder.

A mixture of fear and desire wafts from her body.

Walking down the hall, I carry her to my bedroom, then set her on the floor.

The comforter and top sheet hang off the bed. Grabbing a corner of the bedding, I yank it across the mattress.

Looking up, I find her taking in the room.

"Uhm, I seem to recall someone stating the occupants of this house were tidy?" She lifts a brow. "Housebroken, even."

The floor, covered with discarded clothes and shoes, paints a different picture. Not to mention, several glasses line the dresser and television stand.

"I wasn't expecting company today," I chuckle.

A small smile dances across her lips. "I can see that."

"But in my defense, I wasn't expecting to be almost run over, either, or surrounded by Wiccan covens, brethren, and other clans."

"You didn't just say that." She runs the tips of her fingers over a track trophy, and then inspects the metals hanging on the wall. "You didn't tell me, you run track."

"Well, it's not like we've had a whole lot of time to sit and talk about stuff. Well, normal things, but I'd like to."

"As in a date?" A smile plays on her lips. "Like a movie and dinner date? Or even a dance date?"

"Yeah." The end of year spring dance at school comes to mind. "You're gonna go to KC High, right?"

"KC?"

"Kensington Cove. It's the only public school in town."

"I suppose so." She puts one of the cross-country metals around her neck.

"Then we can go to the spring dance."

"I'd like that." Standing on the tips of her toes, she returns the metal to its resting spot on the wall. "Something normal sounds good."

The elephant in the room, *time*, continues to tick, counting down to the enviable.

Mine, the wolf within whispers. *Mark, Sadie Reed.*

"Dawn is almost here." My mouth tingles, and my teeth shift under the gumline.

"I know." Stepping over shoes, she sits on the foot of the bed.

"Are you sure about this?" Anticipation builds, making my skin buzz with energy.

I've never marked anyone—never wanted to before. But as Sadie said back on the road, *'Never say never because there's a first time for everything.'*

CHAPTER TWENTY-ONE

Sadie Reed

"Am I sure? Yep." I trace the paisley design of the comforter with the tips of my fingers. "Are you good with it?"

"Uh, yeah. My wolf has wanted you since first encountering you on the road."

"That's your wolf. What about you?"

"We are one and the same, me and my beast—the wolf."

"Okay." Taking the hem of the shirt in hand, I pull it off, exposing my pink sports bra. "But do it quick."

He slides next to me on the bed and brushes his lips against mine. The act, simplistic in nature, offers reassurance.

"Ready?"

I nod then ease the strap of my bra partially down my shoulder, exposing the marks left by Keegan and Cole.

Earlier, fear had dominated my mind, but now, there's a calmness around me. One I hadn't expected.

"Mine." A low, throaty growl escapes his lips.

He presses his lips to my neck, then continues the journey down to the shallow marks, leaving a wave of heat and goosebumps in his wake.

"Sadie," his voice is thick, desire-ridden with lust. "May I mark you? Do you consent?"

"Yes," I whisper in his ear. "I do."

Tipping his head, he exposes elongated canines, and then pierce my warm and inviting flesh.

Drawing back, I take in the three small circular wounds. They form a perfect triangle.

"Did I hurt you?" A raspiness etches his voice.

I shake my head then kiss his lips. "No. Actually, I kind of liked it."

"Did you now?" His brows shoot up.

"It was different with you." A yawn plays upon my lips.

"How so?"

"Not sure. I can't explain it."

"Try." He tucks some hair behind my ear.

"Before, in the living room with Keegan and Cole, I was scared, nervous. I didn't know what to expect."

"Oh, and you did with me?"

"No. It's just that I know you'll never hurt me—not willingly, anyway."

"Neither will they, Sadie. The clan members will defend you with their lives. I hope you know that."

"I do now. So"—a grin dances on my lips. "What else does your wolf want to do?"

"More than mere words could ever explain." He nuzzles my neck. "And just so you know, we—me and my wolf—plan on showing you daily."

"Does this mean that I'm yours now?" Well, for the next two years, and then another choice. "That I'm Shoshone? That they can't take me away?"

"Yeah. It does—on both accounts. And I'm yours."

He playfully nips at my lower lip.

"Hey, what's with you and the biting, boy?" I pat his head then scratch behind an ear.

"Yeah. Real funny." Pressing my back into the soft folds of the mattress, he nibbles on my neck again.

His laughter lightens my heart, but an uneasiness tugs at me, refusing to relinquish its grasp.

"Tell me what's on your mind?"

"What if they come for me, Samuel and his coven?"

"Let them try." He ushers a low, throaty growl. "And just so you know, it'll be a wintry day in hell before I let go or allow anyone take you away from me. You. Are. Safe. Sadie Reed."

Worry mixed with fear bubbles in the pit of my belly. "I hope you're right."

"Don't worry." He kisses first one brow then the other. "You're Shoshone, and we take care of our own."

Turn the page for a sneak peek of

COLE
Kensington Cove Book 2

written by

April A. Luna

EXCERPT OF AVA (BOOK 2)

Cole Cotter

THE BAR IS GENERIC and offbeat. Brown carpet, stained with food and drinks, runs the length of the floor below the grooved counter.

Sitting on a wooden stool, I sip the soda in my hand.

The overhead television flickers.

Glancing up, I peer at the screen then turn away, uninterested in the basketball game that's in overtime.

The clock on the wall behind the bar reads eleven-thirty. It's still early. Curfew isn't until two.

Down in the pit, the lower section of the bar next to the live band, Tessa Johansson serves drinks and nachos. The table she's at is full of lycans from the Kweo clan—my inner wolf can smell them.

Most of the faces are unfamiliar, but one stands out, Chad Sawyer. And from the looks of things, he and his squad of brainless followers downed some alcohol before hitting the bar.

Alcohol and Chad are never a good combination in any setting because the idiot can't hold his liquor. And now, here at the bar and grill, with a group of his brethren, well, he's just a fight waiting to happen.

Tessa looks up, and her eyes meet mine.

A smile dances across her lips. She makes her way over to the bar and stands next to where I'm sitting.

"Hey, Ethan," she shouts over me. "Table three needs a house special for three with waters."

Behind the bar, my brother, Ethan, grabs three water bottles and a beef nacho plate with all the trimmings. "What else you need?" He sets the items on a tray then looks at Tessa.

"That's it. Unless you have something that'll take care of stupidity. God. I don't even know why Chad comes her." She rearranges the bottles then nudges me with her elbow. "Hey. You stickin' around?"

"Maybe." I swig the last swallow of my drink. "We'll see. Why?"

A grin dances across her face, and her brown eyes light up. "Because I have a surprise for you and Ethan."

My eyes rake up and down the length of Tessa's lean body, which is poured into skin-tight jeans. An Alpha Prime T-shirt—advertising the bar & grill's fall specials—hugs the curves of her full breasts.

"You ever think of wearing something else?" I shake my head. "With those guys in the pit, you're just asking for attention. The kind you don't want."

A few months back, after homecoming, he and Tessa dated for a while, which was a wild ride.

I came to the conclusion, she and I were better suited to be friends than a couple, and she agreed.

"What? Are you my father or brother now?" Tessa rolls her eyes. "Besides, I make better tips with what I have on."

"I'm not even touching that comment. I'm just saying."

"Yeah. Yeah. I heard you." She turns around and heads back to the pit.

"So, what's going on with Tessa?" Ethan wipes the bar. He picks up the empty bottle, and then he hands me another drink.

"Don't know. She said she had a surprise, and with Tessa, that could be almost anything." I scan the room, which is full of familiar faces. "Seems like a third of the town came out tonight." I stretch, working out the kinks in my shoulders from a hard day's work on the construction grounds I work at part time.

"Yeah." Ethan shrugs his shoulders. "They're either here for the band or the game." He points at the television.

Off to the left, Tessa pulls a tall, young female, well, taller than her five-foot, three-inch frame, into the hallway next to the entrance to the bathrooms.

Tessa motions for her to stay put then dashes off into the kitchen.

Light blond hair pulled into a ponytail, cascades down the middle of her back. She's wearing a long-sleeved T-shirt, sweats, and sneakers.

There's a logo on the shirt. But with the way she's standing, I can only see a fraction of it, so I can't make out what it says.

Shouts, followed by a thunderous boom, reverberates from down in the middle of the pit.

I spin around on my stool, taking in the evening's entertainment.

Two guys, lycans sitting at the table where Chad was

earlier, exchange blows. They flip over a table behind them, knocking over a pitcher of tea in the process.

The bar owner, Isiah Mesnikoff, who is the Alpha of the Black Foot clan—and one of his pack members, his son his son, who is my age—approach the men and drag them outside.

Swiveling back around, I grab my drink.

"Two more Kweo clan members who can't get their shit together." Ethan dries the counter. "It seems their numbers are on the rise."

"What are they doing here? Why are they even at Alpha Prime? I thought they only frequented Adam Lanka's burger joint, Howl at the Moon, in the Kweo region of town."

"Well, you haven't been here for a while."

"That true."

Ethan leans over the bar. "But since Sadie and I got together, the Kweo have become a regular fixture here. Seems they like keeping tabs on me."

"Are they keeping tabs, or are they looking for an opportunity to even a score?"

"What's that supposed to mean?"

"It's no secret the Kweo didn't like the way their brethren's deaths were handled at the Novak ranch." I take a swig. "And they damn sure have made it clear they don't recognize the union between you and Sadie. They think she should be turned over to their clan."

"Well, they can think whatever the hell they want," says Ethan with a low, throaty growl. "But Sadie's mine. And I'll take any of them out who thinks otherwise."

"So will I, little brother because Sadie is Shoshone now. She's one of us."

"Damn straight."

A high-pitched voice cuts through the noise of the room. It has a familiar ring to it.

I scan the area.

Down the hall, leading toward the bathrooms, I spot Tessa, the blonde, and Chad Sawyer.

The wolf in me stirs. I slide off the stool and make my way over to the hall.

Two Kweo members, both lycans, step out in front of me.

"There's nothing to see here." One of the guys says. "Turn around."

"Get the fuck out of the way," I growl. Looking past the lycans, I keep a watchful eye on Tessa and her friend.

"Come on, Chad. Stop it." Tessa's voice quivers. "You've had too much to drink."

Cole pushes past the first guy. But he comes eye to eye with the second, who smirks.

"I'll tell you when I've had enough." Chad brings a flask to his lips and takes three long swigs. "Now. Which one of you should I fuck first tonight?"

I shove the second guy, who reeks of alcohol. "Move."

He staggers back, regains his footing, and then he takes a swing at me.

Ducking, I deflect the oncoming blow then jab with my right.

My closed fist makes solid contact with the guy's jaw, producing a cracking sound.

Behind me, Ethan and the other guy grapple.

"Fuck," I say under my breath.

Keegan told me and Ethan to keep a low profile, and this is anything but low.

"Damn. Keegan's going to be pissed." Repositioning my

stance, I keep Chad and the girls in view while dealing with the Kweo engaging me.

Tessa pushes by Chad's arm, which is blocking her exit. She gets halfway past him and then is slammed against the wall.

"Stop it, Chad." Tears fill her eyes but don't spill over.

My wolf issues a low, throaty growl.

Raising a leg, I do a front kick, connecting with the man's knee.

The guy falls to the ground whimpering, and I take off running toward the girls.

Keegan's gonna be more than pissed, so I might as well make the most of the situation.

I didn't start it, but I sure as hell intend to finish it. And at this point; I'd like nothing better than to beat the fuck out of Chad because the lycan can't seem to get his shit together. Plus, evidently, the dips hit doesn't know how to take *no* for an answer.

Yeah. The lycan needs to be taught a lesson.

Chad grabs the blonde. "I think I'll fuck you first."

She takes hold of his hand, rips it free of her arm, and then she twists his wrist back.

"What the fuck?" Chad falls to his knees. The flask slips out of his other hand and bounces on the carpet, spilling the contents. Face red and eyes bulge, he grunts.

Approaching, I visually examine the hold the blonde has on Chad's hand.

Hell, she knows what she's doing.

"You ever touch either of us again," the blonde says, barely above a whisper, "and I'll break your arm. Are we clear?" She pauses. Her voice is calm and steady. "I expect an answer."

"Fuck you—you bitch." Chad glares at her. "Is that enough of a fucking answer for you?"

"Let's try this again." The blonde twists his wrist back a bit more.

Chad's head bobs up and down. "Yeah. Okay." His response comes out more of a whimper than words. "I didn't want your skinny ass, anyway," he says, barely above a whisper. "So, get the fuck off me."

The blonde looks up. She glances at me then turns her attention to Tessa. "You okay?"

Tessa nods but doesn't verbally answer.

My wolf can smell Tessa's fear, which adds fuel to the raging anger building in the pit of my stomach. She might not be blood-related, but she's like a sister.

"Now, apologize," the blonde demands.

"Fuck you." A fine mist of spit sprays the air. Chad lunges forward, swinging his other arm.

Footsteps pound behind Cole.

"I'm gonna kick your ass." One of the two guys from earlier charges.

"Look out." Tessa's eyes widen, and her brows shoot up.

Spinning around, I deflect the oncoming guy's approach, flip him over, and then slam him to the ground.

"Stay down." I narrow my eyes, keeping him in full view.

"Wrong answer." Without relinquishing her hold, the blonde twists out of the way of Chad's oncoming assault. "You're either not very bright, or you're not listening."

She sweeps Chad's feet out from under him, and he crashes to the floor.

"You shouldn't have done that. I warned you. You should've listened."

A distinct popping sound resonates down the hall.

Chad screams. "My arm." He rolls into a tight ball and cradles his elbow to his chest.

The girl takes Tessa by the hand and leads her past Chad. Together, they walk to the bar, and she helps Tessa slide on a stool.

I approach the bar with Ethan on my heels.

"You okay?" The blonde brushes a loose strand of hair out of Tessa's face and hugs her.

"I'm good." Tessa's eyes fill with tears that spill over to her freckled cheeks.

"What the hell is going on?" Isiah plods to the bar. He studies Tessa's face then hands her a napkin.

Isiah's gaze trails down the hall to where Chad is still on the floor, rolling in pain.

The two Kweo members kneeling over him rise and then head for the exit.

"Go. Take care of that." Isiah motions to Eli, who makes his way over to the injured man. "Someone going to tell me what happened."

"Chad," Tessa says between sobs. "He brought a flask and had too much to drink, again." She rubs her arm, which is red and splotchy. "Why do you even let him in here? He's a dick."

"Hey, Isiah. I'm gonna take him over to the clinic," shouts Eli. "Then I'll drop him off at Adam's place. They can deal with him there."

Isiah turns a hot, burning gaze on me then Ethan. "What the *fuck* are you two doing? I know you're aware of the agreement."

"Hey. Don't look at us." Ethan shakes his head. "We didn't start this. And we've damn sure been upholding the truce on our end."

Isiah narrows his eyes. "Who took the first swing?"

"It wasn't them. They were just trying to help." The blonde steps forward. "And that guy's arm, it's not broken. His elbow just needs popping back into place."

"Keep talking." Tension pulls the skin taut on Isiah's jaw.

"He grabbed Tessa by the bathroom and started groping her. We asked him to stop, and when he didn't, I subdued him. I told him to stay down, but he refused."

Isiah looks from the blonde to Tessa. "You okay?"

Tessa nods.

Isiah takes Tessa by the hand and draws her off the stool. "Get your stuff, and go home," his voice has a softer tone to it. "I'll pay you for the rest of your shift."

Tessa hugs Isiah then turns to the blonde. "Give me a minute, and I'll be ready." She takes a couple of steps then stops. "Hey, Ethan. Cole. She's the surprise I was talking about earlier." Tessa grins, but her eyes still contain remnants of tears. "Can you guess who she is?"

My gaze travels to her shirt. *Johansson's Martial Arts Studio* is written in bold lettering across her breasts.

I glance up. Bright, emerald green eyes hold my gaze.

She looks familiar. It takes a few seconds but then, recognition finally sinks in.

The tall blonde, with the kick-ass moves and lean body, is Tessa's kid sister, Ava Johansson. And from the looks of things, she's not so little anymore.

A grin stretches across my face.

Sucking in a deep breath, I dine on her alluring scent.

Mine, the beast within whispers.

I nudge Ethan. "Seems little Ava can take care of herself." She's a woman my inner wolf now has in its sights.

ABOUT THE AUTHOR

Michelle L. De La Garza is an American Freelance Writer and Poet, who lives with her husband and children in Texas. She writes sweet New Adult and Young Adult Fiction under her real name, Michelle L. De La Garza and writes steamy Adult Fiction/PNR/Science Fiction/Fantasy under pen name April A. Luna.